POTOMAC
review

Editor-in-Chief
JULIE WAKEMAN-LINN

Senior Poetry Editor
J. HOWARD

Poetry Editor
ROBERT GIRON

Managing Editor
STEPHEN BESS

Administrative Assistant/Webmaster
OM RUSTEN

Associate Editors

NASREEN ABBAS
DIANE BOSSER
GENEVIEVE CARMINATI
JEANNE MORGAN CASHIN
PHILLIP CLARKE
KATHARINE DAVIS
SWIFT DICKISON
LISA FRIEDMAN
KAROLINA GAJDECZKA
DORY HOFFMAN
ALISHA HOROWITZ
JAMES LACY
MICHAEL LANDWEBER
MICHAEL LEBLANC
KATEEMA LEE
CAROLINE LEVINE

DAVID LOTT
IAN SYDNEY MARCH
MIKE MAGGIO
SEAN MORAN
SHANNON O'NEIL
WARREN REED
LEIGH RIDDICK
MICHAEL RYAN
JESSIE SIEGEL
JARVIS SLACKS
KATHERINE SMITH
LYNN STEARNS
MARIANNE SZLYK
SAMANTHA VENERUSO
EDYTHE WISE
HANNAH ZAHEER

Interns

TODD KILLICK
MARC CULLY

DAVID MCGOLRICK

Published by the Paul Peck Humanities Institute
at Montgomery College, Rockville, Maryland

The Potomac Review has been made possible through the generosity
of the Montgomery College Foundation.
A special thanks to Dean Carolyn Terry.

Paul Peck Humanities Institute
51 Mannakee Street, Rockville, MD 20850
Copyright 2013

For submission guidelines and more information:
http://www.montgomerycollege.edu/potomacreview

Potomac Review, Inc., a not-for-profit 501 c(3) corp.
Member, Council of Literary Magazines & Presses
Indexed by the American Humanities Index
ISBN: 978-0-9889493-2-4

Subscribe to *Potomac Review*
One year at $20 (2 issues)
Two years at $34 (4 issues)
Sample copy order $10 (Single issue)

Cover Photography by Philip Friedman

Table of Contents

She Tastes Everything First

Nandini Dhar

Grind the posto/poppy seeds to a fine powder

Morning sun brushes the lips of night—
a shy young lover   slow   inexperienced
my mother unlocks the kitchen door
stove   pots   pressure-cooker   saucepan   teapot
spoons   and   cups
quiet as the tongue curled behind the teeth

Cut the potato in cubes and soak in water, else they develop black spots

she reaches for the spoon   names them:
tea leaves, three spoonfuls
water, eight cups of it
sugar, only in four of them—
once the tea has brewed over,   half a spoonful in one
one spoonful in one   two spoonfuls in two
milk, in three of them
one of them, no sugar

Heat oil in a kadai. Mustard oil is preferred.

On the cement countertop a gas stove
on the floor the old kerosene stove   in ten minutes all
three would light up
cooking dal   vegetables   fish stew   all at once
Behind her, the slit of a window
a view of the street ahead—busses, trucks, cars fly past:
my mother chops onions facing the soot-black wall

in the balcony   my grandfather drinks his tea
        smokes bidis with Satyendadu   our neighbor
they mourn   *bangal women could make meat curry out of plain*
                        old grass

Add the whole jeera/cumin seeds and wait till they splutter. You can
add 2-3 dry red chilies too.

        My mother chops onions facing the soot-black wall
            the grass streak of light through papaya leaves
                    green dances   on her face
                tears streaking down her cheeks
            she does not wipe them off   my mother stops
                    lays down the knife
        lifts up the end of her sari   fans herself
unbuttons her blouse

Add the potato cubes in the oil with a pinch of turmeric powder

                    she unbuttons her blouse
            the recycled pickle-bottle of cumin seeds
                the measuring spoon   she lets it slip
                    scratches the skin of her wrist
                six cumin seeds on the kitchen floor
            my mother sticks out her tongue to lick
        the ladle: that's how she checks the heat of the sizzling
                    fishstew every day

Sauté the potato pieces lightly till they develop a golden tinge. Do not
over or deep fry them.

    My grandfather likes to talk about my mother's love for us
            she loves us so much that she tastes everything first
                My mother lifts a green papaya

holds it against the light
by its stem   digs   her thumbnail
into the green of the skin
with the milk oozing out   thinks   for a moment
this is a new beginning
like her nipple oozing milk   birth   only it is not

Add the posto/poppy seed paste.

She squeezes the lemon into the cabbage
one two three four   counts
a sweatdrop dances on her nose   falls into the stew
one two three four   stirs the wok
mutters *stop for a second or two and what we'll have are brown
cabbage bits stuck to the bottom*
inedible   she mutters   *ei, come and scratch my back for me*
she calls me in
yes, there … and down…down…yes.. now leave…
get your homework done
my mother continues to mutter   in the porch
my grandfather sits in his easychair
solves crossword puzzle   needs his third cup of tea
hollers   no one knows if my mother hears it or not
she mutters

*Cook on medium heat till the paste has uniformly coated to the pota-
toes. Stir occasionally.*

Her hair tied back in a bun   she stops   her knife   her
ladle
to look out of the window   the corners of her fingernails
vegetable-juice black
the lines of her palm   yellow   disobedient turmeric

my mother's mother had taught her once
my mother didn't ever need a recipe book to cook   neither would I
she mutters
to the papaya leaves
outside

Add little water (around ¾ cup), adequate salt, and the chopped green
chilies. You can sprinkle very little sugar if you want.

My mother peels the bottle gourd   elongated white sticks
chopped fine   she gathers the skins
in the leaf of her palm   one by one   throws them away
no daughter of mine grows up eating rubbish vegetable skins fish
scales goat bones   at night   mustard oil leaks into my pil-
low   urges me to recreate the faded genealogies of grease
my grandfather and Satyendadu keep talking
about lost cuisines   my mother mutters

Cover and cook till the potatoes are done. Wait for the water to dry
up.

She grates the coconuts   sprinkles the white dust into the
boiling dal   stirs   tells no one
in particular   *this is called folding in*
cuts her index finger   beads of red in coconut's white
she does not shriek in pain   shouts the roof off our house
one day I will let loose these gas ovens   set this whole house
on fire sure I will   I bite
the stalk of the green chili   I had stolen from my mother's
basket   hoping   I will find
the fragrance ma says they add to a stew   surprised
when I find heat occupying my tongue
bit by bit

*At this point you can add about 1 tsp of mustard oil and stir well
before you remove from heat. Take care potatoes don't get mashed up.*

She repeats to herself all our favorites
my father loves coconut sweets   me stew curried chicken legs
my grandmother mango pickles   my aunt fish in nigella
seeds
my grandfather ilish in mustard sauce   she tastes
everything first
discards if they are not good enough   my father says
this is because her love for us is so big that it cannot be measured
I don't know how much   she loves us   what I do know
she tastes everything first   because some things she
wants to avoid   the frown on my father's face   the
sound of the stainless steel bowl   banging against the wall
the lotus of my grandfather's fingers
around the edge of the bowl
before he throws it away.

Counting by Threes

Heidi Willis

Brian glanced at the caller ID and excused himself from the meeting, the suited men around the table frowning as he closed the glass doors behind him. There'd be hell to pay, he thought, gathering his briefcase and coat, but nothing he could do about that.

He scraped the ice from the windshield, then punched at his Blackberry and waited for the heat to kick in. "Kinsely, where are you?" He pressed the phone to his ear as if that would make his wife pick up. "You can't keep doing this."

He considered calling her therapist but his office was closed by now. He'd tell him to wait, anyway, that she'd come home, to make an appointment then, that she needed to decompress; it's not unusual for this to happen, he'd say. In families like yours, it's not unusual at all.

The main roads were dry, but the back roads still slick, and he worried about Kinsely as the car fishtailed rounding a curve. There was always the possibility it could be car trouble or an accident keeping her, but he hated himself for wishing it was something so easily fixed.

The bus lane was long empty when he pulled up to the school. Before he could get out, Gavin's kindergarten teacher swung open the office door and coaxed his son into the cold. The boy shrunk inside himself, a wisp inside the bulk of his coat, only his eyes visible, peering out above a superhero red scarf wound round his face. He stopped at the curb, head bent. A dark stain spread across the thigh of his Superman pjs. Brian glanced at the teacher.

"Right before you got here."

Brian nodded and knelt in front of his son. "Hey buddy. You have a rough afternoon?" There was no reply, not that Brian expected one. "Is it okay if I hug you?" The boy shuffled forward, and Brian gathered him into his arms. Gavin smelled damp and pungent, but instead of drawing back, Brian squeezed his son harder, Gavin's body stiff against him.

"I'm sorry," he said to the teacher. "I don't know what happened to his mom."

"I tried to call," she said, and wrapped her arms around herself.

"The service around here isn't very good," he said. He ran his fingers over Gavin's back. "The mountains... you know." She nodded and shivered. "Okay. Well, thanks," he said.

He fetched a blanket from the back of the SUV and wrapped Gavin. "Can you get in yourself?" he asked, and, met with silence, held out his arms. "Can I help you?" Gavin let his father hoist him into the vehicle and buckle him into the booster seat. The lights around the school flickered, glinting off the last cars in the lot. As they left the school, he watched Gavin in the rearview mirror, straining against the buckle, beginning to rock, his fingers flapping against his knees, ONE two three ONE two three ONE two three. Kinsely had created a chant to go with the rhythms, as much to calm herself as him. MOMMY daddy me MOMMY daddy me MOMMY daddy me, she'd whisper in his hair.

He turned on Bach, the same CD they'd duplicated for each car and his bedroom, and Zuill Bailey's Cello Suite No. 1 filled the vehicle. Gavin stilled.

In a few minutes, Gavin's eyes closed. Behind them, clouds built one upon another, heavy and grey over the mountains. He turned his headlights on and the first flakes splattered on his windshield.

He tried Kinsely again, but the two tenuous bars disappeared as he descended into the valley. She'd probably be home when he got there, quick with some excuse. A doctor appointment that ran late. Some road detour. Burying yet another family pet.

When they arrived, though, the garage was empty, the house quiet. Leaving Gavin asleep in the car, Brian checked the answering machine and the counter for a post-it. The fridge magnets held nothing more than the week's grocery list and the names of prescriptions to be refilled, two for Gavin, three for her. He tripped on a boot in the washroom and kicked it into the dryer, the metallic clang ringing behind him.

He navigated the clutter next to the passenger door, the birdhouse Kinsely's latest addition, next to the fish tanks and hamster Habitrail. No matter what pets they bought to urge Gavin out of his private world, they never survived the household long.

He left another message for Kinsely. "Where are you?" he said, gathering his coat, briefcase, his long-empty coffee mug and dumping them on the washer just inside the door. "I've got Gavin. The weather's turning. You should get home." He hung up and returned to the car. The wind had already blown small drifts over the threshold into the garage. He leaned in and unbuckled Gavin, tucking his scarf under his chin, his son's chest rising and falling. He left both the car door and the laundry door open for Gavin, who would trudge in when he woke.

In the kitchen, Brian unpacked Gavin's backpack, rinsed out the thermos and put the Ziplock of cut apples in the fridge. He wiped the lunchbox clean and was placing it on a dishtowel to dry when he heard his son. Still bundled in his coat, rubbing his eyes, Gavin stabbed his finger at the pantry.

"What's wrong, Gav?"

The boy crossed the kitchen and picked up the lunchbox, putting it back in his dad's hands and pointing to the pantry again.

"Oh, right." He slid the lunchbox into the empty spot next to the box of individually packaged Lays Classic Chips.

Four o'clock was snack time – creamy peanut butter on Club crackers and a box of raisins – but today it was well past four, and Gavin was already leaving the kitchen, finding the recliner in the family room and curling into a ball in the chair, sucking his thumb and rocking, the tang of urine around him.

"Hey, what do you think about a bath? We could dump your whole bucket of dinosaurs in with you." Gavin stopped rocking and bobbed his head. Brian held out his arms and Gavin climbed into them.

While the tub filled, Brian double-checked the rooms, just in case. Once, when Kinsely hadn't made it to the school, he found her asleep in the guest bedroom, pajamas on, hair loose around her face. She'd seemed disoriented when he woke her, but insisted she'd just laid down for a nap and forgotten to set the alarm. Why had she put on pajamas, he'd asked. She'd shrugged, but stayed in them the rest of the day.

But the rooms were empty, the beds neatly made, the vacuum marks in the carpets undisturbed. When he returned to the bathroom, Gavin sat on the lid of the toilet, still dressed as Superman.

Brian tested the water with the back of his hand – not too hot, not too cool.

"Let's get those clothes off you. Did you sleep in those last night?" He'd gotten in late, and Gavin had been, as usual, so far buried under the blankets that he'd had to peel them back just to feel for a cheek to kiss.

Brian reached for him. The boy jerked away, crossed his arms and brought his knees to his chest.

"You put your arms in your shirt," Brian sang in almost a whisper. Five years of the Sesame Street song and it never failed. "You put your arms in your shirt. It won't even hurt." He knelt before the boy, waiting. "You put your legs in your pants." Gavin unfurled. Brian kept singing, "You put your legs in your pants and you'll be doing a dance." His hands fluttered over the clothes so lightly the boy couldn't feel the pressure of them. "And that's what's best about getting dressed." Slowly Gavin relaxed and let his father peel the pajama top off, lower the bottoms, and lift him into the tub.

Gavin smacked his hands flat against the water, droplets spattering Brian's suit pants. "Okay, I remember." Kinsely kept the bucket with the plastic dinosaurs – 113 of them – under the sink, but when Brian searched, they weren't there. Gavin began to cry. "Do you know where Mommy put them?" Brian asked, looking around the bathroom. "Can you help me?" Gavin answered with shrieks, more smacking, water flying. "Give me a sec, okay? I'm looking," his voice tight and too loud.

Gavin's room. He'd often snuck the dinosaurs there, no matter how often Kinsely told him they were strictly for bath time.

"Did you take them to your room?"

Gavin flailed his rail-thin arms against the water, the waves splashing over the side of the tub. "Stop it!" Brian yelled. Gavin froze.

Brian took a breath. "I'm going to get the dinosaurs, okay? I'll be right back. Look at me. You want the toys? I'm going to get them, but you have to stop acting out. Okay?" The boy didn't meet his eyes, but his arms gave one last smack and sank beneath the water. "Good man. I'll be right back. Stay on your bum, okay?"

He dashed out of the bathroom; seven long strides to Gavin's room where he found the bucket beneath the easel, camouflaged by Rubbermaid containers of watercolors and paintbrushes and washable markers. He snatched it and hurried back before Gavin could decide to get out.

Brian shook the toys into the tub. Gavin relaxed, playing with dinosaurs he could name by genus, and Brian wondered what his laugh would sound like, just once, a boy's giggle as the spinosaurus loped across the soap dish, oblivious to extinction.

The sun was setting, but Brian could still see fat flakes flying sideways and back again through the small window above the tub. A bolt of lightening shot across the sky, illuminating the street below. When the thunder followed, Gavin screamed, Brian instinctively reaching out for him and Gavin shrieking louder, thrashing at the touch. Brian held his hands up, his shirt soaked.

"It's just noise, Gav. Thunder, remember? The angels bowling?" He couldn't remember Kinsely's song for storms.

He looked at his watch. She'd never disappeared this long before. "I'm going to get my phone, okay?" Gavin stopped screaming but now rocked, his body creating waves. "I need to call Mom. Why don't you get out for a sec. Sit on the rug until I come back." Gavin continued rocking, hugging himself, water sloshing over the side of the tub. "Or go with me. I can carry you in the towel." He pulled Gavin's favorite dinosaur towel off the rack, the one with a hood and a tail with green spikes, and held it out. "Don't you want to be a stegosaurus for a minute or two?" Gavin scooted closer to the wall.

Brian considered his options. Finally, he rolled up his sleeves and dunked his arm into the water, rescuing a handful of dinosaurs. "I'll be right back. Stay there and play, okay?" Brian squatted until his thighs cramped, and finally Gavin stilled and reached for the toys, his fingers grazing his father's palm. He hugged them close to his chest.

"Okay then," Brian said, and hesitated a moment more before hurrying down the hall, taking the stairs two at a time. The phone was not on the counter where he usually left it. He checked the top drawer, the kitchen table, the top of the washer, fumbling through the items he'd left there earlier.

The kitchen clock ticked off seconds.

The car!

He jammed the phone into his pocket and took the steps three at a time, pulling himself on the railing and spinning around the banister, only to find Gavin smiling. His son held out a plastic Muttaburrasaurus and shook it. "Rawr!" he said.

"He looks awfully fierce," Brian said, breathing hard.

Brian sat on the commode and turned on the phone. He wiped the steam off the screen with his sleeve and turned on the fan. Gavin pressed his palms to his ears, keening.

"Okay, okay," Brian said, flipping the switch. "It's off. No more noise." He cracked the door, and slowly Gavin lowered his hands.

Brian dialed Kinsely's number as Gavin line up the dinosaurs along the edge of the tub, not by color, or by size, but alphabetically: allosaurus, apatosaurus, brachiosaurus, ceratops, dilophosaurus, iguanodon…

He left yet another message for Kinsely, this time just asking her to check in so he'd know she was safe, followed by a text. *Call me!* He checked the forecast next. The one to two inches initially predicted now were blizzard conditions, the pass expected to close before midnight.

The lights flickered.

"Maybe we should end the bath early, kiddo. Looks like the power might go out on us."

Gavin showed no response, the line of dinosaurs lapping one side of the tub and onto the other.

"We could order pizza for dinner. What do you say?"

Gavin continued the march of raptors.

When Brian reached for him, slid his hands under his son's arms, Gavin shrieked, pummeled Brian with his fists. The more Brian tried to hold him, the slipperier he became, until his thrashing wrenched him from Brian's grasp and Gavin's head cracked against the faucet and he fell back into the water. Brian slid on the wet floor, his hip connecting with the sharp corner of the sink. Gavin's shrieks became sobs, and Brian let out a cry of his own.

"Okay, okay. You can stay. It's all right." He rubbed the sting in his hip. "Let me see your head." There was no blood, and that was as close to checking as Gavin would let him get.

The lights blinked again, staying off for a few seconds this time.

Brian pulled a towel off the rack and rubbed it over his hair and sopping shirt. He rested his elbows on his knees, his head in his hands. He took three long, deep breaths before saying, "We need flashlights before it gets too dark."

Gavin rubbed the back of his head.

"Does Mom keep any upstairs?"

Gavin nodded and pointed to the linen closet. Brian forced a smile. "Perfect."

He found two Maglights in an emergency kit with bandaids and Betadine, but neither worked. "Does she keep batteries up here?" he asked, but Gavin was intent on scooping dinosaurs from under the water where the tussle knocked them.

Brian opened the door and stepped into the hallway. There were cabinets to the left. He had no clue what Kinsely kept in them. The first two doors yielded a dozen containers of playdough, a handful of plastic cookie cutters, some paintbrushes. He peeked in the bathroom to check on Gavin who was scrubbing a megalosaurus with his washcloth. In the next cabinet, Brian found a box of cinnamon-scented tealights, two pillar candles, and a box of matches. He grabbed the pillars and matches and went back to the bathroom just as the lights fizzled again, leaving them in shadowy dusk.

He struck a match but as soon as he'd placed the first candle on the back of the toilet near the tub, Gavin grabbed it in his fist and plunged it into the water.

"No!" Brian said. He snatched the candle from the water and slapped Gavin's hand. "You can't touch these." Gavin began to cry, but Brian ignored it, trying to dry the wick and relight it. The flame wouldn't catch, and he blew the match out as the fire touched his fingers. "Now look what you've done. We've only got one candle left."

The boy waved his hands in front of his face.

"I know it's dark. I can't help that. The storm made the lights go out." He lit the other candle and put it on the windowsill, the yellow light bathing them both. Gavin smiled; a victory, Brian thought.

"Five minutes more, okay?"

Brian checked his emails. Nothing.

He was staring at it when the phone rang, the music bouncing off the tiles on high volume. Gavin screeched, covering his ears. Brian fumbled turning it on.

"Kinsely?"

Silence. Then, "It's me."

"Where are you?"

"Outside Pittsburgh."

"You're in Pennsylvania?" More silence. "How the hell did you get two hundred miles away?" Gavin's eyes grew wide. Brian lowered his voice and moved to the doorway. "What's going on?"

"I don't know. I was going to the gym after I dropped him off at school, and I missed the exit."

"And you just kept going?"

"Yes."

He waited. "But you're coming back now?"

"I don't know."

Beyond the window, snow gathered on the trees, weighing the limbs. "Is it the roads?" Gavin had run out of room along the edge of the tub and was now standing in the knee-high water lining them on the towel rack. Brian gestured at him to sit, but Gavin ignored him. Pinching the phone against his shoulder, he grabbed his son's elbow and guided him into the water, waving off his pout.

"Stay on your bum," he said.

"What?" Kinsely asked.

"I'm talking to Gavin. When will you be home?"

Another flash of lightening lit the clouds, and a great rumbling shook the house. He would never get used to thundersnow.

"I don't know if I'm coming back."

"You mean when? Tonight? Tomorrow?"

"If." Her voice was small, far away. "At all."

Brian watched his son flapping in the water, knocking the plastic animals off the side by species, genus, alphabetically, of course. He stepped outside the bathroom and edged the door shut to nothing more than a sliver of candlelight.

"Kins?"

He could hear her breath, a deep sigh that led to a shallower but longer one. "I'm so tired."

"Did you call Dr. Lin? Any of the people from support group?"

"Three years, what good has any of it done?"

Brian pressed the heel of his hand over his eyes. "Come home, Kins. We'll get you help. A stronger anti-depressant. We'll get you sleep pills. Whatever you need."

"You think everything has this simple answer. A fix. A pill. It's not like that."

"You think I don't know? Christ, Kins, where do you think I've been the past three years?"

"Where *have* you been?"

"When I took the partnership, we agreed –"

"You don't know what it's like being with him, all day, every day," she said. "This morning I combed his hair too hard. His *hair*, for Christ's sake. I put too much peanut butter on his sandwich. I ran out of orange juice to wash down the BuSpar. I dressed him in a shirt that's too scratchy."

"And I left work in the middle of a meeting because you weren't there and now I've probably lost my job," Brian said.

She didn't answer.

"Come home," he said. "We'll figure this out."

She let out a long breath. "Figuring out isn't working. I can't do this anymore."

"We're all exhausted. It isn't just you in this family. Jesus, Kinsely," He slammed his hand against the wall. He could hear the tiny plunking of dinosaurs diving into the bath, followed by the wail of his son. He put one hand over his open ear, feeling that this must be how Gavin felt sometimes. Too much noise.

"I should just go."

He lowered his voice and took the phone into their bedroom. "Take the night off, Kins. Hell, take the whole weekend, but do not run out on us." The snow stuck to the window, a thick layer obscuring any view. The thunder reverberated and Gavin screamed, one sharp cry.

"I'm just done," Kinsely said. "It's better. Not just for me. For you and Gavin."

He drew the curtains closed and flipped the light switch, forgetting the power outage. "What do you mean?"

"I killed the parakeet."

"What?"

"Chico. He didn't just die. He wouldn't shut up. He chirped and chirped and made so much noise, and Gavin started screeching which made the bird go nuts, and I shook the cage. I was angry, Brian, and I shook the cage until the stupid bird shut up."

He hesitated. "I'm sure it was an accident."

"You're not listening, Brian. I killed the bird. If I –"

"We'll get you more help," he said. "Another doctor. A specialist to come work with Gavin."

But she wasn't there. The blizzard had knocked out the signal.

He was halfway down the hall when he realized how quiet it had become. He felt his way across the carpet, his fingertips on the wall, feeling for the doorknob, pushing the door, the brush of it across the bath rug, the lingering smell of smoke.

"Gavin?" There was no splashing, no humming, no galumping of dinosaurs across the shampoo.

He blinked in the darkness.

He reached towards the water, finding only air.

"Gavin!" He plunged his hands into the water but came out empty.

"Gavin?"

A whimper in the corner made him turn. He took a quick step.

"Ow," Gavin said, the sound of his voice so human and articulate that Brian froze.

"What did you say, Gav?"

"Ow," he repeated, holding out his hand for his father to see.

Brian opened his phone and held up the bluish light towards his son. The outstretched palm was already blistering. He looked at the trail of water from tub to window, the doused candle on the floor between them.

"Did you touch the fire, Kiddo?"

Gavin curled his hand back into his naked chest, protecting it with his other arm. "Ow," he said.

"Let's get you wrapped up, okay?" He found the dinosaur towel and held it out for Gavin. His son scooted across the wet tile and let Brian wrap it around his shivering body. He began to rock, and Brian pulled him into his lap, wrapping his arms around him like a vise, the kind of pressure Kinsely insisted calmed him. Gavin's body trembled and Brian took up the rocking with him.

Back and forth, ONE two ONE two ONE two.

"DADDY you DADDY you DADDY you," he whispered in the dark.

He'd be here all night if needed. Until the electricity came on. Until the phone signal returned. Until Kinsely came home.

She just needed time. They all just needed time.

No Longer Tell The Crumb from Its Shadow

Alec Hershman

By morning the keenness of loathing
had been replaced—a junco
spilling a bit of purple on the window.
What could she want with my kitchen?
Because it was bright and winter
shadows laid the bricks early,
stark in the good health of their shapes.
Not a cloud. And the little machines
in that house made their whirring
like a membrane as the children
once made—a partial vanishing
beneath the stormy orbit of the bickers.

The furnace on its even keel
filled me with something clean
and glassy as remorse. The bird
tearing service berries
with a little tantrum of its head
was fickle to my eyes. My hands
distracted me with purple too,
more robust, more tumbled
by water than brushed by wind,
but anchored, anchored
where my flightless elbows
refused to bend. And the mountain
was a biscuit at which we ratcheted
and laid the tattoo of our appetites.

The Great Mutual Surprise

Marge Piercy

My own fragility astounds me.
I see myself running up a mountain,
dancing all night as partners fell away,
digging a long furrow and then another,
hiking all day into deep woods.

One flight of steps has turned steep.
I teeter carefully on patches of ice.
The groceries are definitely heavier.
Sleep flirts and may lie down or toss
its heavy curls and slip away.

I pet my kitten wondering if she will
outlive me and I must think of her
future. A will molders in a drawer.
Friends lie under stones or wait
while cancer gnaws their organs.

I still imagine I can do so much
more than I can do. We are all
so surprised by aging, as if we
alone would jog along intact
into some easy flaming sunset.

Springtime

Elizabeth Kate Switaj

buds break—
an agony of seeds
     in cream & pink

   these trees are wanted
I am not

there is no other breed

White House of the Confederacy

Elizabeth W. Jackson

It's as though the house shrinks from the sidewalk,
columns like vertical ribs sucked in, breath held, walls

gray like the skin of the renal patient who plods past.
Wheelchairs and baby carriages swarm the walk;

men with cigarette skin in brownish jeans and women, ample
with worry, flow from parking lot to sliding glass doors.

Tailored suits and Walmart specials skim past
the dull brass plaque of the Confederate Museum

into the hospital that swells around the old house.
My mom, fogged by anesthesia, sleeps in the tower,

her private eighth floor room overlooking
the other side of Richmond. She tells the interns

about her last trip to Sicily, the glory
of Taormina's cliffs, how she hobbled

with her bad hip. She calls for nurses like most
pump buttons for morphine, waiting for ease

before she tries to stand. Only her handsome surgeon
inspires her. He butters her waffles, says "Let's go,"

and she takes her first steps, a debutante
escorted to the ballroom of a hospital hall.

Already, she's already planning for opera in Prague,
espresso on the Amalfi coast, but for now, her maid

will do, staying overnight, plumping her pillows,
holding her arm as my mother grimaces from walker

to tub. I wonder at the beauty that makes me forget
porcelain teacups of presumption, the lips

my mother purses at our Black mayor,
how her eyes slice across the fleshy midriffs of girls,

their belly button rings glinting. I'm always on the outside
looking in, retreating to the other side of the street,

remembering the glamour, how it beckons,
an open window— a party suffusing gold.

2012 Poetry Contest Winner

Mendelssohn

W.F. Lantry

~Elijah: An Oratorio with Words
from the Old Testament (Op. 70, 1846)

I'll always carry matches with me now.
Though I'm no priest of forests or of hills
they have my sympathies, they don't deserve
to have their sacrifices overlooked
or burnt by unseen hands disparaging
their loves, their passions or their revelries.

The chorus, in angelic black, descends
into the pews, the walls are stucco white
and hold unfigured crucifixes, bare
of any suffering, but voices call
in harmony for every Baalist priest
to be cut down, by swords, beside the stream.

And so, with all of us, by stone or flame,
or sharpened gleaming edges flashing down
in choruses of mockery revered
only by gathered ravens, who would feast.
No benefit of orchestra or voice
could reclaim what our ecstasy reserved.

Our act is over. Near the sacristy
the singers gather in their chaos, flutes
and cymbals passing near us without sound
as unfamiliar exultations weave
black robes together, threatening the wind
with wingbeats sharpened on Elijah's gold.

Art Thief

Karen McPherson

I stole away from the studio
with that painting of yours
in my pocket. You thought
it was still hanging on your wall,
but I'd already carried it off
with me in my little glasses
case. I wanted it –
so my eyes took it
and now it's
mine.

Whatever wall I turn to,
there it is.
Scribbled copper fieldscape,
thumbprint sunburned marigold,
magnified whorls and ridges
rubbed out flat.
I see your terra umbra ground
to fine powder for the wind's
bold strokes. The tumbleweeds
tangled in a barbed wire fence.

This world writes over
and over along the same horizon
line. Forest of calligraphy,
India paper sky.
The fluttering pages
of an open book, the miracle
that reading was before you could.

Watching Hummingbirds at Cedar Creek Lake, TX

Lucas Jacob

A cobwebbed morning chill.
Cracked leaves drift from the ash

at the stilled water's edge,
and the first hummingbirds'

little dance begins. A
tentative darting in,

a flight back to shadowed,
spidery branches. This

continues, unbroken,
for a lazy, watched hour.

Of course, the feeder is
manmade. But, then, so is

the lake that drew us here.
So much energy spent

to keep ourselves aloft,
our efforts audible

over gentle breezes
only to those who hold

their own breaths long enough
to themselves to hear ours.

The Craze for Waving at Strangers

Ethan David Miller

"She's not a waver," David said. He drew slowly on his cigarette. It was the third Tuesday in September. A cool fall breeze shook the branches of the trees that lined the main hill. Below us spread all of campus.

"She'll wave," I said. The woman wore a dark pea coat. Her graying hair was pinned back. A canvas bag hung over her shoulder. Just then, she was in the Lake Street crosswalk.

"Wave away," he shrugged. David was lanky and pale. He wore baggy paint-splattered corduroys and an oversized yellow rain coat. He shrugged like a marionette with all his strings pulled at once.

I waved. I made one wave, and then another. I waved back and forth. The woman looked up at us. We were perched on a high, small landing at the back of the Humanities building. It had rained the night before, and the concrete was rimmed with a glossy gray sheen. She squinted a little, her face furrowed in confusion.

"Nope," David chuckled.

I waved more vigorously.

"Nope," he snorted a little this time.

Then, just as she was nearly out of view, the woman turned back, looked over her shoulder and gave me a little one-handed salute.

"Ha!" I said. Then I began to impersonate her. I did my best librarian voice. She looked like a librarian. "I know that short girl with the dark, curling-cropped hair and the bandana," I said, meaning me. "I know her from somewhere."

David laughed. His whole body shook when he laughed. I liked to make him laugh.

"She looks too skinny." I continued my impersonation. I

was too skinny. I barely weighed a hundred pounds. "She should eat more. And why does she keep pulling her sleeves down over her wrists?" I eyed David. I wanted him to ask me about being skinny. I wanted him to ask me about my sleeves. But also, I didn't.

David narrowed his eyes for a moment. He didn't quite see what I was getting at. "I didn't think she would wave," he said.

"I knew she would."

"How?"

"Some things you just know." I gave him a quick look, and then a nudge. Our hands touched. I felt the warmth of his skin against my skin.

It was David who had invented the game. Twice a week after our art history class we would stand on a landing at the back of the Humanities building. There wasn't much to the landing. Accessible by a fire door at the end of a long labyrinthine hallway and a twisting maintenance ladder, it had two broken chairs, a French dictionary, an ashtray and a 'no smoking' sign. "It was built to greet a staircase they never finished," David once conjectured. He was full of conjecture. I had followed him there the first week after class because he looked interesting and I wondered where he was going. After that it became a game. We would smoke, talk and try to get strangers to wave back at us.

"Are you going to Chicago in May?" David asked. "Like all the seniors." This was early October. We were in sweaters.

"I just got here," I said. "I'm a sophomore." He raised his eyebrows in surprise. David, I knew, was a graduate student. He was getting his MFA in painting. He was taking the art history class for special credit.

"Were you at one of the satellite campuses last year?" It was common for students to start at one of the satellite campuses, bring their grades up and transfer in.

"Not exactly," I said. I had been the valedictorian of my high school class.

"What then?" He leaned in. He had a little red stubble on his chin.

"It's a long story," I said. I was glad he asked, but I wasn't ready to tell him. "Pick someone," I gestured to the people passing below, meaning for him to wave.

By the middle of October, I was thinking about David more and more. I was looking forward to our cigarettes. I would wake up on Tuesday and Thursday mornings and lie in bed, and he would come into my mind. I'd think of things to say to him and imagine what he might say. Oh Becky, I thought to myself, you have a crush. I wondered if he had one, too.

Of course I knew David was married. He wore a wedding ring. "What's she like?" I asked.

"Who?" This was the third week in October. The cold had come down from Canada. The leaves were blazing orange.

"Your wife."

"Oh, I don't know," he said. He had a funny, startled look. He was from Kansas. His father was a minister. When I caught him off guard, he looked to me like a minister's son, full of earnest charm. "She's very …" He paused for a minute. It was a happy pause. I could see he enjoyed thinking of her. But then he turned solemn. His lips thinned as he spoke. "I think she thinks this whole painting thing will blow over."

"Blow over?" I asked.

"I used to be a real estate broker before," he said. I knew he was 29. "Cece thinks I'm going to just drop out and go back to real estate. Like this is a phase or something."

"What do you think?"

"Sometimes I think I was better at that than I am at this." He gestured to the paint on his pants.

"Don't quit," I said. I took a drag from my cigarette. "You should do what you want."

"I wish," he began but didn't finish. He looked down at the campus spreading below us. I could see he was thinking. He frowned.

"Don't get serious on me," I said. "Wave at someone, would you?"

That previous spring, things with me had been very touch and go, and I had only decided to enroll in the University at the last minute. My parents and I had picked it because it was close, so my father wouldn't have to jet out to the East Coast if there were problems again. Also, there was in-state tuition to think about. My mother had made clear they weren't paying all that money for another transcript full of drops and incompletes.

So although there were tens of thousands of students on the campus, I had to dodge people I knew from my neighborhood. I nearly ran square into Hannah Farber on Observatory Drive. I had to duck into a bathroom to hide from Lisa Schulman on my way to sociology class. It got to the point that I would avoid restaurants, bars, going out at all, so I wouldn't have to explain what I was doing there, what had happened to me. I wasn't ready to tell them.

Meanwhile, through the fall, the craze grew. Our after-class cigarette breaks doubled from 15 minutes to 30 minutes, and then doubled again to nearly an hour. On a nice day, we would stay all afternoon, just leaning, standing, smoking, talking. We shared a love of anomie, Frank Lloyd Wright, and the engravings of Albrecht Durer. We hated crustaceans, Woody Allen movies, and decorative fonts. All the while, we waved. The craze grew in our minds, too. It became a quiet, enveloping volume like the smell of cinders on a summer wind.

Like all things, the craze had found rules for itself:
1) Only one-handed waves were allowed.
2) Don't push David about his marriage.
3) Don't push Becky about her past.

When the past came up, I told David I would tell him next time. It became a joke. When I looked long at David's wedding ring, he looked at me very seriously. It was not a joke.

Over the weeks each of us had our memorable victories. For David, there was of course the first victory, a man in a brown coat. Later he had scored a girl with a tennis racket who had made a big arching wave and an older lady with a shopping cart who had waved back with both hands. On Halloween, David had scored a man in a gorilla suit and two people dressed as burritos.

"Those burrito people are waving at everyone," I said.

I had my own successes. There was a young woman with a ponytail in a tracksuit who had waved to me the third week, put her hands to her mouth and hollered, "Hey!" as if we had been old, great friends. There were a couple of men – university people, city workers, alumni. I sometimes wondered how David felt when I waved at men – was he paying attention? Did it even matter? If I picked a student, and he waved back, I would try to catch David's eye – was that twitch jealousy, or was he just twitching?

The first Thursday in November we were standing out on the landing, and I spotted a boy I knew. "We went to high school together," I explained to David.

"You can't wave at him," David remarked matter-of-factly. "Only strangers."

"I've known him since kindergarten," I added. "I know his sisters and his mother and his father. They go to synagogue with my parents. "

David realized we weren't talking about the waving game.

"Oh, don't worry, I'm avoiding him," I said. "I'm not going to wave at him." A gentle drizzle was falling. Drizzle was worse than snow because it soaked through everything. "I'm not supposed to be here," I said. "I don't want to have to explain myself to him. There are a lot of people from my high school here. I don't want to have to start explaining to everyone."

David considered me. He grinned faintly. "That's a feeling I can understand." He inhaled gently on his cigarette.

The boy walked out of view. Soon it began to rain a little harder. We finished our cigarettes and quickly ducked inside.

That Tuesday, David looked terrible. He had bags under his eyes and his whole body drooped. It seemed like he hardly had the strength to stand.

"I don't know about this whole thing," he said after lighting my cigarette and then his.

"What?" I was frightened he was talking about me.

"I just had this horrible critique," he said. "You know I've been painting my ass off, and nothing is ever any good."

"Do you think it's not good?" I asked. "Or do other people think it's not good?"

"I can't tell the difference anymore. I think Cece thinks it's not good."

"Do you like doing it?"

"I love doing it. It's the only thing that makes me happy. It's who I am."

I frowned.

"This makes me happy, too," he added quickly. "I could shoot the shit with you forever."

"Listen, if you love doing it, you should do it."

He started to speak and then stopped. He started again, but stopped again. "Thanks," he said. "It's nice to know at least one person feels that way. It's nice someone believes in me."

Then he smiled. He looked like he was just about to kiss me, but he didn't. I couldn't get that look out of my mind.

The next week, the last of the leaves fell from the trees. They were everywhere. Overnight there had been a cold rain, and in the morning, our landing was slippery with an autumn cake of leaves and ice. David broke up the ice and swept it away with a broom he found so I wouldn't slip. I rubbed my hands together to keep them warm.

We were out for a quick round during the bathroom break in class. He pointed to a woman on the sidewalk below. She was, I noticed, very pretty. Almost alarmingly pretty.

He was baiting me.

I nodded. I shook my hair. I feigned disinterest. I told myself if he was baiting me, it was because he liked me, because he needed me. He wanted me to react, to confirm. I was stoic. I flashed him an indifferent look. You're stuck in this, too, I signaled.

David pulled off his glove with his teeth and moved his wrist with a tiny, gentle motion. The woman saw him. She looked to our spot high on the leaf-covered hillside. She was a looper. She made a wide gesture with her arm. Somehow it was a flirtatious wave. It was the posture of her body, the arch of her spine. David smirked with satisfaction.

I felt a pang of jealousy. I shook my head.

"I'm sorry," David said.

"Sorry for what?"

"This is a shit show," he said. His smile broke for a moment. He leaned against the chair. He looked exhausted and in pain. "I keep trying to stop this, but I keep making it happen." He looked at me and at his ring and at me again.

After class, David asked me if I wanted to get a coffee.

"Sure," I said. I felt weak in my legs.

"Where?" He shouldn't have asked where.

"My kitchen," I said. I was stunned by my own brazenness. I was surprised that the words came from my mouth.

David's eyebrows lifted. He was on the defensive. I liked it. I felt smart and pretty. I pushed my hair behind my ear.

We walked up the windswept path that wound around the side of the lake. We tried to speak, but our voices were lost in the howl tearing off the gray water. We crossed a broken flagstone patio and entered the old Victorian I shared through a storm door. Somewhere along the way, we had started holding hands. We did not stop in the kitchen. We did not brew coffee.

It happened in my small twin bed. Outside, the last migratory birds were heading south for the winter. Afterwards, he looked at me expectantly.

"What?"

"Well?" he said.

I didn't know what he meant. Then I did. "You want to know how it was?"

He blushed.

"It was nice," I said. "You're nice," I said. "I wish you hadn't kissed my scars." I had long scars on my arms from where I had slit my wrists the year before.

He blushed redder.

"Oh, I'm sorry," I said. "I didn't mean to be mean. Just to be honest."

He nodded.

"Okay," I said. We lit cigarettes. I told him my story.

"I'm sorry," he said. "I'm sorry that happened to you. I'm sorry you tried to kill yourself last year."

"It's nothing," I said. "It's all in the past. I'm making a new start here. It's just sometimes I feel like a total pariah. I feel like I don't have a place in this world."

"You know, you don't have to be perfect. People will accept you for who you are. I do."

"Thanks," I said. "If you mean that. If it's not just something you're saying to be nice. Because you slept with me."

David nodded. He was wearing his corduroys but no shirt. The little pile of hair on his chest was the same rust color as his stubble.

"You know, I know, like, a million people here. From my neighborhood. From high school. I know they know. Everyone knows. I don't want to have to explain." I paused. "I don't know where I belong," I said.

David leaned on the windowsill and looked out over the freezing lake. Over the semester, he had grown from thin to thinner. I could count some of his ribs.

"You've gotten so skinny," I said. I knew it was the art and Cece and me. "When I'm with you, I feel like I belong. Do you think we belong?"

David drew hard on his cigarette. The paper crackled and the radiator banged. "It sucks when you say things like that." He was suddenly angry.

"Why?" I asked softly.

"Why," he said, his voice full of scorn and hurt and maybe self-loathing. He threw his arms up as if he was asking the lake. After a long moment, he began to speak. "Cece and I have a son, you know. He's three. I'm a father. I have responsibilities."

I nodded, but I felt dizzy. I hadn't expected that.

"I am so fucked," he whispered to the icy water. A moment later, when he looked at me, his face was masked in a laconic smile. He began pulling on his clothes. We kissed goodbye.

That next week, I tried to kiss him when we were walking down the little hallway to our landing. I looked back behind me to make sure no one was watching. Then I leaned in, and pushed my lips against his lips. He turned his face away.

"No," he said quickly.

"What?" I asked.

"Before was a mistake," he said.

"A what?"

"This isn't what you think," he said. "I mean, it is what you think."

We stepped out onto the step. The sunlight was abundant and cold.

"Cece and I met in high school," he began.

I nodded.

"We fell in love. I thought she was the most beautiful person I ever knew. She has this wonderful laugh, like a coin rolling around in a jar." I could hear how much he loved her in his voice.

I lit a cigarette and offered him one.

He shook his head. He needed to say what he was saying. "She's real quiet. She grew up on a dairy farm. It's no joke about the work."

"Anyway," he said, "it doesn't matter. So we were in love, and we got married." He was so uncomfortable. He shifted his weight from one leg to the other. He was shaking. His face was twisted in a grimace of pain. "I guess I thought that if I tried hard enough to be someone I could become that person."

"But you couldn't." I shivered against the cold.

He shook his head no. "I'm stuck." He continued, "She's not like you. She's not vulnerable or smart or funny. Sometimes I just sit in my chair in my studio, trying to draw, and I compare the two of you. Or actually, trying not to compare you."

"You don't have to be stuck."

"Yes, I do."

"You don't." I reached out to hold his hand. He didn't take it.

He thought for a moment. "I think you're doing this because you know I can't really be with you. You're just figuring shit out," he said.

"Me?" I said. "I think I'm doing it because I love being with you. I love talking to you. " I began pacing the small landing.

"No." He thought for a moment. "You don't belong here. You don't belong with me. You're like too –" he stopped in the middle of his sentence.

"Crazy?" I said. I was hurting. My head throbbed. I could barely follow the conversation.

"I don't know." I saw him scan the street below. He stroked my hand. "You're too you."

We sat out there for a long time.

The last week in November, David had an art opening. It was for all the graduate students at a gallery in the Humanities building. I was terrified of running into someone I might know. Becky, I said to myself, you can do this, and I went.

The gallery was just down the hall from our classroom. All the work was on the walls. A woman poured white wine. A cellist played. I spotted David's work right away. I recognized the colors from the paint stains on his pants.

He had seven or eight paintings — abstracted visions of different parts of town. Each was marked by a dramatic and unusual perspective. I understood what had first drawn him to our landing.

Beside the arrangement of pictures was a ribbon. In spite of his gloomy talk, he had won second place. At first I thought there was nothing of me, or anything familiar to me in the paintings. Then I realized there was a painting of the lead gray water of the lake, the tops of trees in the foreground. It was a sad picture, full of shadow. It was the view from my bedroom window.

"Whoa." I exhaled hard and felt an urge to leave. However, when I turned around, there was David and his wife and their little son in a stroller on the other side of the room.

She was small and blond, but she was not prettier than me. I had come knowing this might happen – in fact wanting it, but not expecting it. Everything was suddenly real.

David saw me. His eyes widened. He looked trapped, terrified.

I waved.

His look narrowed. He pretended not to notice me.

I waved again.

His wife glanced at me, leaned in to him and whispered something.

I approached. "Are those your paintings?" I asked.

"Yes," David nodded. He wore an expression of sheer panic.

"I really like the one of the lake," I said. I don't know where my boldness came from. "Though it seems so sad. I wonder," I trailed off. "What vantage point did you paint it from?"

Our eyes locked. He opened his mouth, but nothing came out. A too-long moment passed.

"He never reveals that stuff," Cece jumped in with a little laugh.

"Oh, I'm so sorry," I said. I touched my chest. "I'm Becky." I extended my hand. "David and I have an art history class together."

"I'm Cece, David's wife." She shook my hand. She had no idea. "This is Thomas, our son." Then she picked up Thomas. "Say 'nice to meet you,'" she said. The boy wore a little suit and had on a small tie. They were, I realized, the clothes they dressed him in for church. She smiled. She had a nice smile. She was probably a nice person. "You have to excuse David," she said. He stood slack jawed. "These things make him so nervous."

I nodded at Cece. "I hate all these things, too." I had never been to an opening before. "Do you want to grab a cigarette," I said to David. I was betting she was not a smoker. "Can I borrow him?"

She looked quickly to David. "Sure," she shrugged. I wanted her to stop me. I wanted her to know I was dangerous. She didn't care.

After a moment, David and I were walking down the hallway and up the maintenance stair to our landing. We walked in silence.

"What are you doing here? What are you doing?" he asked as soon as we stepped outside. The cold air burned. I had never been there at night. We lit cigarettes.

"What do you think I'm doing here? I came to see you. I came to see your work." Below us, we could see the headlights of cars snaking along Lake Street. Snow covered everything.

"Becky," he said. "This is fun," he gestured to the landing. "But that's my life," he pointed through the door in the direction of the gallery.

"Fun?"

"Okay," he said. "It's a pit. I'm miserable, and I'm in love with you. And I can't stop. Are you happy?"

"It's not a pit," I said softly. "It's my life."

"This is a game," he said.

What troubled me was how I had made this mistake. How I had substituted a game – a simulation – for the real thing. I knew it then, and I was sick to my stomach. I was ready to retch. "You're an asshole," I said.

He smiled.

"Only assholes smile when you call them assholes," I said.

He looked wounded.

"Okay," I said. "You're not really an asshole. You're just a coward."

I stomped my cigarette beneath my boot and stepped inside.

I hated him. But I understood him. There was nowhere I belonged.

That week something strange happened. I was walking out from the library, and I spotted Hannah Farber. She had auburn hair and a ready laugh, but we had not been friends. I couldn't say for sure why.

I felt uneasy. I wanted to duck out of the way. But I didn't. For some reason, I thought of the craze and thought, I wonder...and before I could finish wondering, I had waved at her.

She walked right over. She was wearing a puffy jacket. "Becky Silver!" she said. She greeted me with a hug.

"Who are you visiting?" she asked.

"I go here," I said.

"Don't you go," she paused for a moment trying to think of the name of the fancy liberal arts college I had burned out of.

"I transferred in September," I said. I felt nervous but also okay.

She smiled. "Well, welcome home, Becky girl!" She gave me another hug. David was the last person who had hugged me. And that was weeks ago. I almost cried. I didn't know how much I needed that hug. She gave me her phone number and her e-mail address. She told me about a party some brother of a boy we'd gone to school with was throwing.

At the party, she introduced me as her friend. She called me Becky girl again. I liked being Becky girl.

There were other people I knew at the party. People I'd been avoiding for months. Some people asked why I had transferred. It was hard every time I answered. "It's a long story," I said. No one asked twice. I was shaky the whole evening, but I did it. I kept looking at the door and thinking, 5 more minutes, 5 more minutes, but I stayed all night.

A guy in a band asked for my phone number. "Don't you know I'm crazy," I said. I made a circle with my finger beside my ear.

"Everybody's crazy," he said.

"No, I'm the real deal," I said.

"Will you give me your number or what?" he asked.

I didn't care if he called. At the end of the night, I got invited to another party for the next weekend.

Hannah and I stood in front of the bus stop at Lake Street. In the moonlight, I could see the landing where David and I stood on the hillside. I could make out the forlorn silhouette of the two chairs and the ashtray.

"What are you looking at, Becky girl?" she asked.

"Nothing," I said. "I don't know. Just something I had to go through."

She was drunk and humming to herself. Then, suddenly, she looked at me. "You know, no one cares." She paused. "I mean everyone cares. But we don't care about that." She was slurring her words a little.

I understood then that she knew. That they all knew about what I had done to myself, what I had tried to do. In only a week word had gotten around. Someone had told her. Maybe the child of a friend of my parents.

"Is that why you're being so nice to me?" I was suddenly viciously angry. I had been terrified of this.

"No!" she said. "No, Becky. I always thought you were so smart. I always admired you. I always wanted to be your friend. You were always so busy. You put so much pressure on yourself. No one could be your friend."

The lamp light above us flickered. I heard a car pass on Langdon Street. I knew she wasn't lying. I had never seen myself that way before.

When her bus came, she gave me a hug and a drunken kiss.

The thing was that David and I did not stop playing.

"Why are we still doing this?" I asked David one day in December. A real hard cold had finally come to the city. It would not budge until April. Snow was piled everywhere. The people passing below were bundled tightly in their mufflers, scarves, hats and boots.

"I don't know," David said. "I think it's habit. We just let habit carry us along."

"What about courage?" I asked.

David gave a little broken-hearted laugh. Like someone smashing a bottle on a curb.

"I sometimes wonder what will happen to us. I mean, after this class is over." I exhaled hard. I was looking for something on David's face. "I have all these fantasies. Sometimes I think maybe you'd run away with me, you'd just forget about your wife and your son."

David nodded. There was pain. I knew he had thought about it. I could see he was nearly in tears. I wanted to hug him, but I didn't want to touch him. I needed to protect myself.

"I used to just think about running away alone. You know, maybe Chicago or Portland. Anywhere," I said. I took off my hat and ran my fingers through my hair, and put my hat back on. "That's the thing about fantasies," I said. "They're not real, so you can go around and around with them forever."

David couldn't speak. What could he say? He shivered. He breathed. We saw his breath. He was ready to cry. We both were.

"Sometimes I imagine," I said. "I think we're up here playing our game. And there's some real good-looking guy walking by. Like all the way down on Lake Street. And I wave to him. But he's not like the other people who either wave back or pretend not to see me."

David nodded. He could see where I was going.

"Instead, he comes up here. He walks up the side of the hill, and he comes up here. And he asks me out. Like right then." I took a deep breath. "The part of the fantasy that matters is not that. I never really imagine the guy with any specificity. What I imagine is you. What would you do? What I wonder is, would you try to stop him?"

David shook his head no. It was a tiny, little half shake. The final diminished bounces of an object coming to rest. There was a bitter wind, and we didn't wave at any strangers that day or again.

The last time I saw David was after the exam. I had a plan to meet Hannah for a drink. David and I walked out together and smoked a cigarette. He told me he had decided to drop out. There was a moment when I wasn't sure if we would hug or not. What I do remember, distinctly, is that as he walked away, I didn't turn, I didn't wave.

Elegy For The Night

Rebecca Parson

In the tangle of day, I walk
among crowds penned in
by the sky's bright fence.
But when the light knots
itself into stars and I see
past them, I'm awake, alone.
And just when something almost
happens, day rises solidly,
as if night says,
I'm not yours.
I'm not yours.

Winter Break

Janet Hagelgans

It's his first Christmas with his sons
home from college, one at the piano, the other
nosing through the pantry, everything

louder than he remembers. His joy
is like the turkey thermometer that plunges quick and
deep, heats up, tells him he's done right. In three weeks

they'll be gone again. He'll unlock the kitchen door when it's
    already
dark. He'll go to the switchplate and hang up his
jacket and take a leak and dry his hands and wait for those

heavy teenaged footfalls to fill the silence
but unlike him the house can
hold its breath forever. He'll touch the dormant piano

and the moulding on the doorways and notice
his life's container has become an object in its own
right, the way when you take a portrait off the wall the paint

is a lighter shade than the rest and you can't help but
stare at that empty rectangle.

Doing Laundry Together

Gabriella M. Belfiglio

The day I leave for school, we go to the 24-hour laundromat—
the big one on Washington. I leave her to the sorting
of clothes, go in search of coffee. At Tom's Diner
people are grouped in twos and fours, a colony
of squawking seagulls gulping pancakes and eggs,
not as lucky as the others
who flew out of the city for the long weekend.
It is the end of summer, and the very air is different
not just in temperature and light, but in people's
breath—a collective sigh clouds over the neighborhood.
I could walk these streets blindfolded.
Every corner has a reminder, like a wrapped present,
of somebody I have loved or hated or both.
I return with the coffee, just the way she likes it—
black one sugar. The clothes are turning in the wash.
When we woke up I lingered longer in bed
than usual; I moved my body close to hers.
I could navigate her landscape blindfolded.
But she insisted there were dirty clothes I would need
mixed with hers and we left the apartment
full of heavy bags.

Vacuum

Alex Koplow

"I'm leaving you," Lorain promises when she catches me yawning in my taped-together recliner. "For the day," she concedes, unbolting the door with a sigh.

I can no longer measure Lorain by her sighs. They are so frequent that they just fill gaps, like exhales or ums.

"I have to go," she vows. "I work."

She yanks the front door shut, and the screen settles behind her. She probably wishes there were more doors to separate us. But they swing open again. From my recliner, I heard it coming, a slight warning from the creaky screen.

"Thom, if I come home tonight," she sighs and looks me in the eye, "and I can see my footprints in the carpet, it will be the last you ever see of me."

The doors shut again, and I go vacuum the bathmat. I carry the mostly-clear, bagless vacuum from the front closet, appreciating its off-balance bulk. There's another vacuum slanted under the bathroom sink with the tampons and plunger. There are two in the closet of the spare room. There's one that Lorain doesn't know about tucked next to the water heater.

Bouncing off the shower's chalky tiles, the vacuum's bass rattles my chest. The noise domes me. Panic from the morning, the way our tension makes Lorain blame me for the sour taste of the toothpaste or the Wi-Fi being slow, evaporates.

When my phone vibrates in my pocket, I'm afraid to answer it. If it's Lorain I'm sure she's calling to divorce me. And the way that every traumatic moment is ingrained, I'll be haunted by the clothes I'm wearing, the vacuum prices on Best Buy's website, and the taste of the blood on my lip from shaving, which I only do every morning so I look less unemployed to Lorain.

Before checking my phone, I vacuum the hallway, absorbing the empty echo. Over the uneven carpet, the vacuum moans like grazing cows. I coil the rubbery cord and hide the vacuum. Peeking at my phone, I see my mom's missed call.

I am honest when she asks me what I'm doing. There is half a response, a noise like she's blowing on hot soup.

"Thom, I don't get why you're still doing that."

Mom is a master of imprecise euphemisms. 'Doing that' has been code for masturbation, dressing goth, marijuana, grad school, soy milk, and now vacuuming.

I offer a watered-down version of what I always tell Lorain, how the vacuuming settles me. I see myself making something better.

"Do you want me to ask Conchita for a lead? She must have a cousin in Los Angeles."

"Mom, I don't want your housekeeper to find me a job. You don't get it."

"Quit acting like I'm so dumb, Mr. Ivy League. You've always done that. Just like your father."

My mom and dad divorced ten months ago. In middle school, when all my friends' parents were separating, mine stayed together, oblivious to the trend. But their single friends kept pressuring them, recommending divorce like it was some amazing TV show my parents missed because we didn't have cable.

'You *have* to try divorce. It's so complex. You can borrow the DVDs.'

Compacting years of arguing into a few intense weekends, they binged on bitterness and legal battles. And there was no one they'd rather share it with than their only child.

Dad didn't want a family. Mom cheated on Dad. Mom sacrificed her body, her career, her life. With amazing frequency, one called to complain while I was on the line with the other. I imagined they could hear each other, the way they'd listen on separate phones when I'd call home during college. I felt like the byproduct of two terrible people.

When I found out they'd split, I was having lunch with Lorain at a café in Santa Monica, and I could barely hear my mom through her coughing and crying. I remember pop songs bursting from passing cars, the creased apron of the cute waitress, and the gross taste of aioli on the sandwich Lorain ordered and made me switch with her because even though she specifically ordered it without aioli, she wouldn't let me send it back because that's rude.

I stumbled back to Lorain's building and asked her if I could sit on her floor for a while if I promised to stay off screen. I ignored my dad's calls.

Lorain teaches at an online military academy. In her small office, several computer screens are broken into quarters, streaming unruly children from around the country. Her cadets are a collection of public school expulsions, eccentric misfits, and children of conservative nuts who wouldn't trust their kids' education to anyone who hasn't killed something.

Lorain snuck into the job because of a year of Junior ROTC she did in high school. She wears a nondescript imitation of a military uniform. From off-screen that day I saw her grainy, blonde students were wearing untucked versions of the same khaki outfit. The Hitler youth associations were unavoidable. But when you're unemployed, Hitler is everywhere. Adolf, *Everybody Loves Raymond*, and that kinda attractive chef with the short arms and huge head. You can't miss them during daytime TV.

Crouched on her flecked carpet, I stared at my phone as it jittered from my parents' repeated calls. They'd tricked me by separating only after Lorain and I got married. It started a countdown for my inevitable divorce.

Lorain didn't have a job when I was diagnosed with testicular cancer. We'd stay up all night at my house, conforming to the odd hours that cancer and unemployment create. Both conditions lend themselves to inventing businesses and bizarre futures, then imagining the minutia of these ideas until they are so real that they are warm and taste metallic.

The goal of The Store That's Always Been There was to make husbands and wives driving around on Sundays say things like, 'Is that place new?' 'No, that store's always been there. See how the sign is water-stained?' 'Oh yeah, we bought that antique lamp there, didn't we?'

But Lorain and I wouldn't sell real antiques. We'd sell things like large coffee tables with crinkled issues of *The Atlantic* attached. We'd customize the little white sticker with your address and a slightly misspelled version of your name.

Stores that have always been there are the best. Scanning our dusty aisles, you could assume that you're not the first sucker to pay that much for a chipped candelabra. We'd sell you a large mirror, come to your house, match the wall color, and put the smallest drip of paint on the edge of the frame to make it blend in.

We'd sell spice racks with one jar missing. We'd sell under-inflated basketballs. We'd sell things that look like they've always been there, things to plug you into the social contract of living in an apartment, having a life, that's smaller than you'd expected.

I vacuum the patio. I vacuum the couches. I vacuum the carpeted floors of the closets. I try on old coats. I do James Bonds in the full length mirror, swiveling and firing the 2" diameter hose attachment at my reflection.

Pacing by the front door around noon, I consider buying a hardwood floor vacuum. The pictures of them online look like hammerhead sharks. I like the idea of pushing around a shark by the tail as it eats dust. It seems like something the Flintstones would do.

I can't remember the name of the guy on *The Flintstones*. The orange and black shirt main guy. I don't know if I've ever actually watched that show.

Straddling an inverted vacuum like it's a bongo, I absorb the gentle pull on my shirt. I eat a sandwich and crumbs get sucked right from the bread into the vacuum. There's a beautiful arc at the end, like the tail of a Q.

"What's up, Jered?" I ask, tapping on his counter to the beat of a song from his old radio.

"The price of gas," he says, pointing to the tower that displays their rates.

Jered is the mechanic I bring Lorain's car to when it makes crunchy noises. A few times a week I walk down to his garage through our Westside neighborhood of straight streets and single story homes. Jered grew up in Maryland, across the Potomac from my Virginia suburb, and we bonded over the ineptitude of DC's sports teams.

When I thought I was dying, I gave him my old Redskins jersey and a box of porn. He misconstrued it as an exchange program and continues to slip me DVDs and website pass-words, always of Asian girls.

We head to the potholed alley behind the station so he can have a cigarette. A beat up sedan crawls by, splashing the puddles in front of us. Like always, Jered's careful to exhale away from me.

"Where'd it go?" He asks, pointing at my crotch with his non-cigarette hand.

"It's gone," I say. "For now at least. It could always reappear."

"Not the cancer. Your nut."

"Oh...I dunno. Destroyed, I guess."

When I told Jered my diagnosis, he repeated it back to me. "Testicular?" he sounded it out with unending syllables, making me realize that the word depends on cancer. I imagined cancer metastasizing in the dictionary, spreading through the red spine and down the pearl-colored page divider, mangling words into 'ovarian', 'pancreatic', and 'adrenal.' Other than cancer and maybe pasta, what could be testicular?

"Destroyed? Like smashed or burned or something?"

"Maybe."

Jered picks at his well-manicured beard. In thick cursive letters, his name is stitched into his shirt. It's a sense of job security that Lorain and I have never had.

"Don't you feel off-balance or weak?"

"Not really," I shrug, but it makes me think I misused my testicle when I had it.

"You should have asked to keep it," Jered says, flicking his cigarette into an oily puddle.

"And do what with it? Put it in a jar on the mantel?"

"Beats me. But you only get two."

"And you only need one."

"Shoulda kept it, man."

My dad's brother, who we think made his fortune illegally, was sure I was going to die. From his own deathbed, he paid for most of my treatment and gave me a heap of money to spend on things he couldn't. Dad told him that my prognosis was actually good, but Uncle Rob insisted. His money let me resign from my position as an Assistant Professor. Looking back, it's caused so much tension between Lorain and me, but, at the time, it was such an obvious decision. I became a full-time cancer patient.

I feel bad. I remember nothing from when I heard Rob died.

But his death vindicated his assurances, like he'd detected something fatal in me that he'd seen in himself. Lorain graduated from UCLA into the Recession and was on the edge of moving home, so I used some of Rob's money to pay her rent. After six months, I moved her in with me. We became very good at being unemployed and dying. In between all her job interviews that led nowhere, she brought me to chemo and doctors and surgery and everywhere I was afraid to go alone. We were two fallen trees that had propped against each other, branches entangled, instead of hitting the ground. I was desperate for permanence, and she needed approval. So we got married. Neither seems like a big part of marriage anymore.

Back at home the sweet smell of vacuuming lingers. But the distractions and unease are returning, so I throw away the mostly ice soda Jered let me have for free and hurry to the bedroom.

I plug in the vacuum and make long rectangles. Each pass tessellates the carpet. The floor glows. Fears of cancer and divorce drown out.

I slide the bed into the corner, revealing brunette clouds of Lorain's hair and our suitcases, carcasses of our honeymoon. Around the house there are framed photos of us splashing in the ocean, initials in the sand, drinking drinks out of coconuts. Tropical beaches rely on girls with bodies like Lorain's. In the photos her stomach is permanently toned and sandy. Her brown shoulders are crisscrossed with tan lines from days of different colorful bikinis. I am skinny, pale, in long-sleeved T shirts and a Nationals hat.

Aside from the pictures what I remember from the trip is the panicked turbulence on the flight back. My sweaty palms against the cloth armrests. Lorain rattling her rum cocktail as a cure-all. The seatbelt sign dinging, then flashing, then no lights at all. A tumbling down the stairs type of shaking.

This is my cancer. Constant buzzing and atonal machines, sounds you can't ignore or locate. It is invisible aching and wrecking pain from within. Obvious details of family, past, and self waft away into the piercing noises. And even when cancer is finally silenced, it feels like at any moment, it will echo.

Vacuuming overwhelms it all. The warm plastic in my hand vibrates. The carpet, the cord, the dirt, all respond to me. Vacuuming creates a tunnel, an impenetrable noise that defends me from cancer, death, and divorce.

At first Lorain was happy to see me up and moving around. She told me how much she liked coming home to our clean, little house and how much she liked coming home to me. Then she got a job, and I got better.

Months passed, and I was always there when Lorain came home to our clean, little house. I sensed her worrying that the house kept getting cleaner and littler. But I'd found so much tranquility in vacuuming that I didn't need her support. I just needed her not to be angry.

By 5:30 I have to deconstruct the vacuuming. Coiling cords and emptying storage bins, I stomp around the house, shuffling my feet over the carpet. I erase the perfect lines and patterns of the bedroom and hallway. It feels like breaking apart a one million piece puzzle. The house looks so ragged. I can't believe that it's how Lorain wants it to be.

The creaky screen warns me that Lorain is home. Grocery bags, the color of old piss, dig into her palms. When I reach for the bags, the static from roughing up the carpet shocks her. It is far from a cute, spark-of-love shock. She is alarmed and annoyed, and I can see her wishing she were anywhere but here.

The smell of vacuuming hovers. She sniffs and sighs and launches in.

"Thom, you need a job."

"I have a job. I clean the house. For you. For us."

"No, you need a job that you get paid for."

"I still have Uncle Rob's money. And you make me dinner. That's kind of a payment."

"I know, Thom. I know what I'm doing for you."

"Come on, Mish." I try to appease her with an old nickname, but the last thing she wants to remember is how long we've known each other, how entrenched she is.

"Vacuuming is a good thing," I maintain. "It doesn't hurt anyone."

I've set her up. She reminds me for the thousandth time how it has hurt someone. Her best friend was at the house watching a movie, and I wanted to show how powerful a new vacuum was by pulling a pretzel from her hand. The tube sucked in her friend's hair and ripped off a clump. I apologized and helped stop the blood and offered to pay for a haircut, but Lorain didn't talk to me the rest of the night. I slept with her back to me, a little proud of how strong my vacuum was.

"I don't deserve this," Lorain pleads into her palms.

She's suggesting that some girl, somewhere, does deserve this. Deserves me and my vacuuming. In my mind that girl is shapeless and ugly. But she becomes blonde. She gets pretty. She is several girls from the past. My mom's friends, ex-girlfriends, and old students. The girls that have always been there.

I mumble something to Lorain about how vacuuming feels like meditation.

She says that when you don't have a job, you don't have stress, so you don't need meditation. I think if the Dalai Lama were living with Lorain, she'd tell him to throw out that stupid toga, put on a tie, and actually *do* something.

I'd swap stories with the Dalai Lama and show him drawings of my ideas for hose attachments (the pitchfork, the anteater, the see-through).

Lorain makes an intentionally bland dinner, willing to punish herself to disturb me. She refuels with red wine, swirling a large goblet over the carpet. She thinks I'm afraid that she'll spill. She still thinks the vacuuming is just some OCD cleanliness thing. I'm more afraid of the vampire look of her wine-stained teeth.

She sighs herself onto the couch, twisting into a position that suggests she doesn't have bones. She is too quiet. This is it. We're over. Forever I'll be stuck with the dry couscous in my teeth, the dish soap stinging my eye, and the ceiling fan's warped reflection on the white tiles.

"Patton called me a cunt today." Lorain confesses, facing away from me.

Patton is a nine-year-old cadet from New Jersey who last week submitted photos of Lorain to dozens of lesbian dating sites.

"Sergeant Cunt," she adds after a glass-emptying gulp.

I rush over to the couch, kiss her cheek, and massage her neck from behind. The stretched chest of her military uniform has little swaths of color, mimicking badges and awards, and a knock-off version of the American flag to be blurred into legitimacy through a webcam. I wonder if there is an online Betsy Ross imitator sewing these.

"How am I supposed to reach these kids when they're half a world away?"

"They're delinquents, Mish. They're programmed to say terrible things."

"I really want to care. But sometimes it's so tempting to shut off the screens and let it all go black."

This is my wife. Our struggles and deficiencies are most binding. I finish loading the dishwasher, and she changes into her old sweats with BRUINS running down the leg. Faint circles of her nipples shine through one of my old undershirts. The tan gap of her stomach and her slanting hip bones direct my attention down. I've told Lorain that she never looks sexier than in her sweats. She always laughs it off, perhaps misconstruing it as an insult to her expensive wardrobe. But it's her stripped down appeal, the comfortable confidence that we are us.

We grip each other in bed. Lorain seems tentative, aware that I'm both the source and solution to her problems. After enough silence that I'm afraid she's going to attack me for vacuuming, I whisper in her ear.

"At least it wasn't Corporal Cunt. He respects your rank."

Lorain doesn't laugh, but she nestles in closer. The way we know how to fit our bodies together reaffirms that we are still those tangled trees. Eventually she spasms, an aggressive leg twitch that happens every night when she's finally asleep.

I owe today's survival to a nine-year-old who attacked my wife from the other side of the country. The days that are the worst for Lorain, the days when her students refuse to give themselves buzz cuts or throw their uniforms over their webcams, are the easiest days for me.

I wake up late, which isn't easy when you don't have responsibilities. There's a wrinkled depression on Lorain's side of the bed. In my boxer briefs, I vacuum the sheets. While the coffee maker burps through its cycle, I see a text from Lorain.

"when are U gonna stop?"

"Vacuuming? When it stops making me feel safe."

"how safe do U think i feel? not knowing if my husbands ever gonna make money. why dont i get safety?"

The distance is reassuring. It's easier to attack when we can't collapse against each other.

"I'd have a lot more money if I didn't bankroll you for so long."

I thought marriage would create a unit, but it's still natural for me to think independently. I'd get so angry at Lorain when she called it 'the' cancer and not 'your' cancer. It was mine. It was in me, not in the. Not in us. Cancer isn't an appetizer or a newspaper that can be shared.

"I will vacuum less. Promise." I type, not because I mean it, but because I need things to be smooth. I text her that I'll cook dinner tonight, too.

After nearly an hour, "no more chicken" pops up. My phone vibrates again. "not spaghetti either i WILL scream if theres spaghetti."

Lorain and I met four years ago at a BBQ on Easter Sunday. She wore an intentionally torn, baby blue shirt that I said looked like it got ripped when she pulled it off a clothes line. Joking that she'd never seen a dryer, I kept calling her Amish. I pretended that she didn't have electricity, demonstrating the propane grill and an MP3 player.

"Let me show you how this works," I mocked, tapping at my cellphone as a trick to get her number.

We cooked burgers and crouched on dirty patio furniture. I was teaching at a small college north of the city, and she still had a little over a year left at UCLA. With eager opinions she challenged my beliefs on the philosophers I taught. Her clever logic and full lips made me reconsider theories I'd dedicated grad school to.

Two minutes before three o'clock, a rolling earthquake trembled through the yard like the patio was driving over cobblestones. The Earth, the most stable thing on earth, was moving and shaking and not doing its fundamental job of sitting there.

"Let me show you how this works," Lorain winked, cracking a beer for me and hoisting one to her lips.

We drank until things felt stable, and then drank our way past that. There's a framed photo on my dresser from that day. Lorain and I are squeezed between two friends, one of whom gave us the frame, engraved with the message, "The Earth

Shook The Day They Met." It's beginning to seem more like a warning than a cute story.

I vacuum the plastic blinds in the front room. They crinkle, the sound of tiny bones breaking. As I grip the ribbed hose, my phone vibrates through the noise. I shut off the vacuum, and the blinds crash against the window. It's my dad calling from back East. He's met another new woman.

"For lunch she made me pasta with marijuana in the sauce. I've been giggling for hours."

Lorain had too much wine one night and swore that because my dad cheated on my mom, I was destined to cheat on her. Cheating is a dominant trait in the male DNA, the English major told me. I argued that my mom cheated on him first, which Lorain only twisted into further proof that I'd stray. Her insecurity is so focused on us that it's comforting.

"Thom, there's being unemployed and there's being useless," he states when I tell him what I'm doing. "Figure out which one you are, and don't let anyone know."

"I improve my surroundings, Dad. And make myself feel better. What could be more useful than that?"

"Oh I don't know. I think I might still be stoned."

"I gotta go, Dad."

"Son, wait. I love you. Being loved, that's a great use."

"Thanks, Dad. Take a nap. It'll wear off soon."

"Good."

With three attachments I vacuum the stairs. I vacuum the tray that divides the cutlery. I vacuum my recliner. Cord in my hand, the vacuum idles until it's so loud that it's finally all there is.

"Price of gas," Jered responds, before I say anything.

In the alley, he lights up. I pace, explaining a hypothetical that captivates me some nights after Lorain is asleep.

"Four vacuums. One on the floor pointed up, one on the ceiling pointed down, and two on the walls pointed in. Turn them on and put a ball in the middle. What happens?"

Jered scratches a dried spot of oil on his shirt with a long fingernail.

"What kind of ball?"

"There is no ball. Hypothetical ball. Hypothetical vacuums," I explain.

"Shit, I dunno," Jered shrugs and leans against an old SUV. "Try it. You've got four vacuums."

Staring at the maze of an undercarriage on his car lift, it never occurred to me that I could. I tell him that I will actually do it.

"Hold up," Jered says, rummaging through a tool box in his office. "You'll need this," he hollers.

He hands me a DVD with a cover of two topless girls facing each other, their spread legs forming a diamond. "It's a weird one," Jered warns as I hurry down the alley.

At the grocery store I pick two steaks for dinner and swing by the produce section to grab ingredients for a salad. I squeeze tomatoes and avocadoes for tenderness, imagining them levitating between my vacuums. I'm about to unload everything onto the checkout belt, but I double back to the alcohol aisle to get Lorain's favorite wine. I hunt through the shelves until I find the import she likes, an unpronounceable cabernet with a Gothic-looking label.

Back at home I assemble my four strongest vacuums in the front room. I turn one upside down and struggle to keep its floppy head pointed up. When I can't balance the vacuum on its curved handle, I secure it to the couch with duct tape. I move two bookcases to the middle of the room, see-sawing them into place by lifting one end at a time. I position two vacuums on top of each squat bookcase, stretch the cords to the sockets, and fire on both switches.

I drag the fourth vacuum over to the staggered noise and uneven tug created by the other three. I lift it in the air, my arms shaking from the vacuum's unstable weight. The cord dangles in my face. Peering into the dark innards of the vacuum reminds me of the barrels of a shotgun.

As I'm envisioning how I'll attach my last vacuum to the ceiling, Lorain walks in the front door. I missed the screen's warning. She shouts something at me, and one by one, I turn off the vacuums. When the noise dies, she picks up Jered's DVD that I left on the coffee table.

"You're home early," I say, because I've heard people on TV say this before.

"This is vacuuming less?" She yells, poking me with the DVD. "What makes you think this is OK?"

"I had cancer," I mutter, tasting the tiredness of the excuse.

He was my fourth doctor in a week. I'd ended those days cowering in Lorain's apartment, spouting facts about wolf populations, golf courses in Africa, Tennessee folk art, and other topics I'd nervously absorbed from waiting room magazines.

His gray eyebrows were like the bristles of a frayed toothbrush. He handed me the paperwork he'd been reading from and continued to speak, interlocking and separating his fingers. The papers were off-white and heavier than normal. Like the kind you're supposed to print your résumé on.

There were three images. The word 'testicular' popped out from the black text. I realized that everything he was saying, this word, these photos, this future, applied to me. The cancer was in my testicle.

Complete recovery had a likelihood of 80-85%. Instantly I felt the victim of that rogue 5%, the most susceptible and indiscernible. Cancer was crawling inside of me, warping my body, spreading like invisible rust.

I asked where it came from. I wanted the cancer to have been a part of me forever, to have my blue eyes and sweaty feet. I wanted the doctor to say, 'Your cancer? Oh, that's always been there.'

"Environmental, hereditary, predisposition," his methodical list prodded me. Everything, myself included, was a suspect.

On the drive home, I deconstructed the diagnosis like it was a car accident. If I'd left the house a few minutes later or made it through a light before it turned red, I wouldn't have gotten cancer. If only I'd dropped off the dry cleaning before my appointment, everything would've been fine. Those clothes, pleated khakis and two dress shirts, were lumped in my backseat for months.

I entered Lorain's small apartment that night and collapsed onto her futon, a creaky leftover from her dorm room. I felt so guilty, like I'd done something to deserve the diagnosis.

"Mish, I have cancer," I recited to her, like it was a fact from a waiting room National Geographic.

In her military uniform, Lorain places the DVD on the ringed coffee table. She doesn't touch her temple, the sympathetic way she usually does when other people tell her they have a headache. She doesn't have a glass of after-work wine from the bottle I bought. Instead of searching the carpet for lines or sighing about her cadets, she tells me to sit in my recliner.

The warm, dusty air kicked up from my vacuuming traps a beam of the early afternoon sunlight. Lorain's khaki shirt is unbuttoned to her cleavage. In my pocket, I feel my phone vibrate. It is not my mom or my dad or an earthquake or my cancer. It is divorce. I am going to remember this.

Apology

Matt Kilbane

Growing up, one crutch the kid had
was saying *sorry* too often, so

it cost him; to break the habit he
paid his mom, each

time, a quarter. Then what
he's really sorry for

went underground, tunneled to
subtext and hunkered there.

The anesthesiologist hadn't
slept for days, settled

exorbitantly with his botched
triple-bypass, but

still wrote an apologetic get-
well-soon card with

cats on the front. In the King James Bible,
the italics cue translational

additions, but you can
read them, and are tempted to,

emphatically—"Blessed *is*
he whose transgression *is* forgiven,

whose sin *is* covered." A sort of
chord then, as mortar

begins to matter. The TV personality,
who while grinning and scowling

both, likewise admits a wrong-
doing and that wrong's

inevitable, sad necessity. At home we
all nod and smile knowingly, say

that's one way to do it. Writing
a poem is another.

Island Time, Aquinnah

Jane Hoogestraat

From the red cliffs of Aquinnah, fragment of shell
salmon-tinged, edged with a hint of dusk, distance
on the face of things, in the face of, expressions
on a face, on a sea coast, where a rock seems animal

like, an imagined swimmer, a fin surfacing gray,
deceptive. Far below, a cove (of thought) opens
a nick of sand, a reflecting pool. The Aquinnah knew,
settling here, how hard the cliffs would be to scale,

no harbor out of vision range, three-sided Atlantic
backed by grassy plains, bluestem, then forests
disappearing over retreating figures, dream
weavers slipping the net's underside.

A scent of sweet goldenrod mingles now
with exhaust fumes from the sickly buses, skittish
over red roads. Fall nights sea lavender light enough
for walking the ghosted coast of native time,

Nantucket still extinct. Aquinnah meaning
"land under the hill" and at times the "praying town,"
sub-clan of the Wampanoag, eastern people of the dawn.
Squibnocket Pond at "the place of the red cliff bank,"

white cliffs stained, tribal lore, with blood of whales.
Early ones arriving on an ice floe gazed at cliffs carved
by a hundred million years, ancient spirits, keepers
of time beyond time, looked up, and called it good.

Pas de Deux, Minneapolis Zoo

Kristin Camitta Zimet

Loosed from gravity, from hunch and lumber,
concrete slapping sole, bark yanking claw,
his thousand pounds forgiven, Kenai treads
water. Forgets the cave, inverted hemisphere
of plexiglass and simulated rock.

Runs in a torpor slower than honey
or a comet's slide. Constellated bubbles spin
around his muzzle. Currents sweep his fur
like solar wind. Below his stretch and swipe
the salmon laze, in sly trajectories.

Sinking, padding up, rounding his pole
with hulking arabesque and tour jeté,
almost he sees into another space:
a wheeled chair, locking brakes, arms
dug by nails; a grizzle-headed bulk

slumped forward. Across her irises,
wide in the dark, the great bear swims.
Slipping beyond her foot rest,
children shift, spangled, indifferent
meteors in a constricting sky.

Sign

Jesse Wallis

Two evenings in a row, as I watered in the garden,
a hummingbird swooped in to drink from the hose

that I held by my side. The iridescent blur of a bird—
garnet crowned, emerald bodied—needled its beak

an eighth of an inch into the top of the stream, drank
there a second, dropped down a few inches, stopped

to drink again, then down once more near the ground
before slowly skipping its way back up, step by step,

following the water's path to my hand. Thirst gone,
it hovered for a moment at eye level and darted off. …

Who knows what meaning flows or flies in anything.
Only, my mind had been troubled for some days—

and there was this bird …

Teacher's Ear

Wendell Mayo

In nothing but a ruby two-piece, Miss Surratt, our eighth-grade English teacher, rose from a green-banded lounger and crossed the deck to a polished aluminum ladder. Fraction by fraction of flesh, she lowered herself into the brisk pool water. My classmate, Maude Roller, ran to the edge of the pool and cannonballed in, creating a small tidal wave that sloshed against one side of Miss Surratt's head. The lifeguard, a kid I knew couldn't graduate high school for the life of him, raised his sunglasses a moment, then parked them back on his nose, folded his arms, and seemed to resume his slumber.

Maude doggie-paddled over to Miss Surratt.

"I didn't know you lived here at the Cooling Pond Apartments," she said.

Miss Surratt squeegeed water from her eyes, replied, "I'm just subletting a place for the summer."

Then Miss Surratt palmed water, faced me. All around her, afternoon sunlight glinted off Maude's residual waves like paparazzi camera flashes.

"Are you coming in?" Miss Surratt asked, squinting.

Was I?

My silence hung like a lonely little jetty running from my mind, over the water, to nowhere. It was summer, 1963, Cleveland, and all that past school year I'd been hopelessly in love with Miss Surratt. I wanted words that would march onto that jetty and enter her ear, but which words? The possibilities were endless:

—Yes, Miss Surratt.

—I'll be delighted, uh, whatever your first name is.

—Sure, baby, I'm coming in!

The possibilities were like white light, how our Biology teacher, Mr. Skulski, had said it was made of every color of the spectrum. And when I mixed every possible response to Miss Surratt's "Are you coming in?" all I got was a kind of white silence. So, towel across my lap, I silently watched her trickle by, short black hair fanned, undulous, like ciliated paramecia I'd seen wriggling under a microscope in Mr. Skulski's class. When Miss Surratt dove under, she appeared shadowlike, seemed to glide beneath a shimmering Pacific while I, her distant lover, observed from some cliff high over a bright California beach. When she climbed out of the pool, a cloud sailed in front of the sun, and, like the dimpled surface of a windy cove, goosebumps rose along her neck and arms, nipples stood high and hard against the fabric of her ruby bikini, and I could just make out the vague cleft of her vagina, at least I thought *vagina* for want of another word, *vagina*, repeated over and over in our sixth-period sex education class by Mr. Doty, whose grimaced delivery made the word sound ugly in my ear. Vagina or not, I was mad about Miss Surratt. When she said things like, "Buck's story in *Call of the Wild* is not just about animals and people in conflict with nature, it is a *call* for social justice," smitten, I believed her, though I had little notion of what *social justice* meant, only that it sounded lofty, like *We the People*, things like that.

When Miss Surratt climbed out of the pool, she clenched her prickled arms under her chest and dropped into her lounger. Maude dropped next to her, flat-chested, shivering, freckled Maude, a kid my mom got me to hang with since she knew her mom from Girl Scouts. Maude's claim to fame around school was raising her eyelids with her thumbs, then rolling her eyeballs all the way down in their sockets so only the whites showed. She said it was her ultimate comeback in an argument. She was a very popular kid at Ford Motor Company Junior High, outgoing, everything I was not.

After a short time, Maude rose, marched over to me, ordered me to get up, then dragged my lounger to Miss Surratt's side. She pointed, a signal to sit. I could see her silently laughing as I lowered myself next to Miss Surratt, all the while pressing my towel over my swim trunks with my elbows in embarrassment. Miss Surratt and Maude shut their eyes tight and cocked their heads back to face the sun.

It was in such a moment, unobserved, that I discovered Miss Surratt's right ear, unabashedly exposed because pool water had pasted her dark hair tightly to her scalp. Her ear's curvaceous, softly canted ridges resembled gentle waves radiating from a single center after a pebble drops into calm water, or, in even larger aspect, a timeless rainbow of geologic layers descending miles into the Grand Canyon, breathtaking, hopeless—how could I ever traverse such distances in time and space? I wanted to pour my heart into her ear—sun and clouds, summer and goose bumps, nipples and glittering water—along with London's Buck and White Fang, how both had somehow managed to endure the brutal cold and wilderness to end up in sun-drenched California—because that was my story, too. That past year I'd suffered lunchboxes drop-kicked in hallways; jockstraps tugged tight into the crack of my ass; the Big Healey Brother straddling my chest, chirping, "Go on, cry, Wiener. Wie-ner! Wie-ner!" After all my tribulations in the vast, wild, icy reaches of Ford Motor Company Junior High, here I was, at last, basking in sun and shadow with the woman I loved—and her magnificent ear.

But how could I speak to her? I rarely spoke in her class. When she'd made us memorize and recite a few lines of a poem, Edith Sitwell's "Dirge for the New Sunrise," the only line I could choke out was, "The living blind and seeing dead together lie."

Which got me a D+.

She explained to the entire class that the poem was about devastation after an atomic explosion, and one couldn't get that from my one line. But while I could see how *Call of the Wild* pertained to me, not so with "Dirge." I'd learned atomic explosions were not so special, in fact, going on all the time, after I submitted five different "current events" articles for credit, all headlined, "US Performs Nuclear Test at Nevada Test Site."

"You have five nuclear test articles," Mr. Yuall, our World History teacher, said to me. "Can't you find something else in the news?"

"But they're five *different* explosions in five months," I said, and managed my best junior-high shoulder shrug.

Silent me, I accepted my C- on all five explosions, without mentioning that my dad had cut the articles out and insisted I bring them to school.

When Miss Surratt rose from her lounger, she stretched a little, then left us. I went over to Maude's apartment at the Cooling Pond. When my dad knocked on Maude's door, she answered. I tried to squeeze past Maude quickly and leave, but she blurted out, "We went swimming with our English teacher!"

"Hmmm," my dad said, the same skeptical *hmmm* he used when he wanted to have the last word, yet keep the matter of me and what he considered my excessive desires open, or perpetually stalled, like my wanting dagger-sharp Beatle Boots and a leather jacket. He was a nuclear engineer at NASA's Lewis Research Center, worked on fast-breeder nuclear reactors for deep space travel, and I suspected the CIA had brainwashed him to keep his lips pressed so hard together that when certain words tried to get out it sounded like *hmmm*.

Once I asked him why space exploration was important.

"For one thing, boy," he replied, "someday, from space we'll be able to deter a nuclear strike—and strike back if need be. We'll have the last word—which means we'll finally have peace on the planet."

That's all I ever got out of him about space. Still, it was more than I'd managed to get out of my own mouth when Miss Surratt had asked me that Saturday afternoon, dolorously, provocatively, "Are you coming in?"

That night, after seeing Miss Surratt at the Cooling Pond, I had my first wet dream. I've never since felt the same sticky mixture of ecstasy, terror, and confusion. I remember trying to picture putting my *penis*, another of Mr. Doty's grimaced expressions, into Miss Surratt's vagina. In class, Mr. Doty hadn't shown that part in full, had only revealed trippingly quick that "the male inserts"—but how? "The male inserts" sounded like instructions for installing my bicycle seat to its frame. I simply couldn't fathom it, legs getting in the way, pushing, but with what? My hips? Come on. And how'd I ever get past the language of a student, "Excuse me, Miss Surratt" or "I'm sorry, Miss Surratt" or "Did I get this part right, Miss Surratt?"

Did one get partial credit in matters of sex?

I spent a long time trying to fit the pieces of that puzzle together, so long I eventually pushed away from it and went to find my dad, who was reloading 30-06 rifle cartridges at his workbench in the garage. Weekends, he exchanged his suits and ties for pleated-pocket rayon shirts and slacks from the 1950s, a time he was in the Navy, the Korean War. He was just starting my favorite part—melting scrap lead in his hotpot. Somehow, his skimming the dark slag off the surface of the molten lead always fascinated me. There was something about the shimmering purity of liquid lead I loved, despite knowing the next step was to pour the lead into the mold to make bullets, destined to be fired, flattened, and tarnished.

Later, I fiddled with my stamp collection, set the garbage at the curb, mowed the lawn. I had a lot of time to myself and so tried to pile all my experiences and imaginings into one concupiscent cornucopia to send straight to Miss Surratt's ear. But everything seemed stupid. Wet cut blades of grass whipped my ankles. The mower throbbed on. So did my heart.

When I went indoors for supper, Maude telephoned me to say Miss Surratt wanted to take both of us to see a special production of *Hamlet* downtown at the Cleveland Playhouse.

"What did you say to her, Maude?"

"I told her I loved Shakespeare."

"What a suck-up."

"Are you going or not?" Maude huffed.

"I'll ask."

After my father's dolorous *hmmm* the week before, I decided to approach my mother about *Hamlet*. I found her in the kitchen where she was making a pineapple upside-down cake. She wasn't aware I was there when she threw open the oven door, seized the pan, and lifted it to cool on the stovetop.

"My English teacher," I said, "wants to take me and Maude Roller to see a play downtown."

With a fingernail, she whittled tiny patches of dried flour from her thumb.

"What play?"

"*Hamlet.*"

I waited a little while, seeing that she was about to flip her right-side-up cake upside-down onto a large plate. I'd always had better success in getting yeses from her at some crucial point of inflection like that, her gingerly tugging at the cake, trying to get it to drop, whispering softly at it, the way she used to whisper at me when I was little.

"Maude's going, Mom," I reminded her.

"Oh," my mom said and tapped the bottom of the hot pan quickly with the heel of her hand. The dessert plopped onto the plate with a smooching sound, its delicate composition of pineapple slices and golden cake unsullied.

She beamed at her upside-down cake, swiped her hand on the front of her apron.

"Mom!" I said.

"Alright, I guess," she said.

When Miss Surratt pulled up in her sky-blue VW station wagon, she already had Maude in the front seat with her. Maude waved me out of the house just as I was adjusting the new cigar-brown dickey I'd managed to talk my mother into so long as I kept it out of my dad's sight. I looked both ways, then dashed out my front door and into the backseat. As soon as I entered the sacred interior of Miss Surratt's VW, Maude started giggling at my dickey. But I sat straight, proud of my new accessory, something that I felt differentiated me from the sea of assembly-line kids at Ford Motor Company Junior High. And I was happy in back. If I could not figure exactly how Miss Surratt and I fit together, if I could not have her man to woman, at least from her backseat I could continue to admire the magnificent pinkish interconnected terraces of her right ear, to me no less a world wonder than those of the Hanging Gardens of Babylon.

While Miss Surratt worked through the gears, Maude babbled on about Shakespeare.

"Which is your favorite play, Miss Surratt?"

"I like them all," she replied.

I wished Maude would shut-up—then I might have a chance of making some perfect sound, set air molecules vibrating in Miss Surratt's ear, create a sympathetic vibration in her eardrum, then she would understand what I felt—not only about her poolside beauty, the frozen sagas of Jack London's creatures and characters, pleas for social justice, but now the fragrant urban miasma of downtown bus fumes, sky scrapers sculpting rhomboidal spaces of blue sky, brooding lower floors of the Midland Building, and higher windows of the Terminal Tower, like sooty hyena eyes, laughing dangerously from tall grasses of the Savannah. But Maude ran her mouth the whole way in.

When we parked downtown and entered the Playhouse, Miss Surratt turned to me.

"Follow the usher," she said.

I led, trailing a shadow and jittering light through a darkly tapestried theater, a softness everywhere, muted, echoic sounds of people settling into their seats. Here was a world within a world, quiet, protected, not jangling like the mower's casing, hot bullets plopping onto my father's workbench, not the assembled giggles and screeches of my Ford schoolmates.

When we reached a middle row on the left side, Miss Surratt smoothed her skirt over her legs and entered first. I followed her straight away, with Maude behind, at my elbow, attempting to sneak past me and sit the other side of Miss Surratt. But before she could slip past, I dropped into my seat and jabbed my knee hard into Maude's thigh.

"Ouch!" she whined and glanced, goose-necked, at Miss Surratt, who, in the dim light held her program at her nose, trying to read. I jabbed Maude again, harder, just as the lights dimmed, stage lights snapped on, and a fog began to roll across the stage. This time Maude jackknifed inward, folded, and fell backward into her seat.

I gloated a long time at my successful pre-emptive strike against Maude. Then I continued my intermittent study of Miss Surratt's right ear. The stage fog created a kind of milk swirling in the dark tea of the theater's interior, which quickly reminded me of the churning lines of a blue-on-white finger painting I'd been proud of at age six—it all seemed part of some grand cosmic plan that, somehow, the same whorls in my finger painting could be found now, eons later, in the tender folds of my English teacher's ear.

I missed most of the play, though my attention was drawn intermittently to references to ears—in *Hamlet*, ears are abused, taken prisoner, sliced in two, and mildewed, not to mention the opening scene when the ghost describes his brother murdering him by pouring poison in his ear.

"Not the ear!" I gasped at that point and Miss Surratt gave me a stern look.

After that, I continued to steal glances at her ear, imagined splitting the stream of utterances from the stage into two parallel flows, one into her ear and an identical one into mine. I observed Miss Surratt's reaction to words pouring into her ear, those that seemed to mean most to her so they might mean most to me. But at only one point did she react visibly. When Hamlet said, "To be or not to be—," there was a hitch in her breathing, an almost undetectable gasp, and by the time the Dark Prince added, "to take arms against a sea of troubles and by opposing end them," I was sure I saw her right eye moisten. But I didn't know what these words meant to her, could not imagine the kind of catastrophic circumstances that could make her react that way.

A couple times I turned Maude's way to see her lips moving in synch with the words, no doubt so she could parrot them back to Miss Surratt in some egregious moment of brown-nosing. For myself, I felt Hamlet himself summed up Shakespeare, "Words, words, words."

When the play ended, people stood and applauded in a haze of momentary adoration. Maude leaned far out her seat, across my body, and addressed Miss Surratt.

"Hamlet is such a troubled boy," Maude said, rubbed her thigh where I'd jabbed it, then snapped back into her seat, turned to me, added, "Don't *you* think so?"

"Yeah," I said and glared at her, "troubled."

While people rose, gathered things, and exited, Miss Surratt sat mysteriously immobilized.

"I won't be coming back to Ford next year," she said. "My boyfriend and I are moving to San Francisco. We're going to graduate school there."

Maude said, "That's wonderful, Miss Surratt!"

Then Miss Surratt turned to me.

"What do you think?" she asked, her tone oddly the same as her 'Are you coming in?' from the enchanted waters of the Cooling Pond.

The lights went up, the maroon tapestried interior of the theater swam, my mind whirred. I felt a kind of centrifugal force ready to fling outward at her ear every beautiful thing I wanted to express to her, the reach and blur of my experiences, my bold imaginings, things I knew would dissuade her from leaving. And what more dramatic venue than the Cleveland Playhouse? I'm not sure how any words at all formed in my brain and got past the dry click I made at the back of my throat—but they did.

"What's his name?" I said.

"Name?"

"Yeah," I said abruptly. "Your boyfriend."

It took a lot to stump a teacher, but I had.

After a few long seconds, she said, "Jim."

"Jim who?" spat out my mouth in thinly disguised vehemence.

It was the most I'd ever said to Miss Surratt.

It was coming out all wrong.

"Alright," she replied, then laughed a little. "James Oates. His name is James Oates. I don't think you know him. He's a mathematician at NASA."

"My dad works there," I grumbled.

"No kidding?" Maude said.

"Really," Miss Surratt added, flatly. "Maybe your dad knows him."

"Maybe," I said and sank back into my seat, regarding her treasonous ear from a distance, remarking to myself how the cursed concentric circles of her ear now looked like Dante's Hell, which Miss Surratt had introduced us to that past year.

Introduced? Now, I'd fallen in, head first, all hope abandoned, clinging to the second circle just above her earlobe, buffeted by cruel whirlwinds of forlorn lust.

The way home, about the time we reached the Brook Park Road exit off I-71, Miss Surratt asked the inevitable question.

"So, do either of you have questions about *Hamlet*?"

"I wondered why," spewed from Maude's mouth, "Hamlet does not slay Claudius while he's praying—but then I remembered he didn't want to send his soul to Heaven."

Of course! Miss Surratt, like the scheming Prince of Denmark, had delayed announcing her leaving all year long to strike now—and send my soul to Hell.

"What about you?" Miss Surratt asked me.

As one of the newly fallen, I only had one question—how to depose James Oates.

"Can you remind me," I said, "of the name of the poison that the guy poured into the King's ear?"

"Hebenon," she said.

"Can you get that anywhere?"

"I don't think so," she replied.

Sometime over the next two weeks, I found my dad at his workbench. He was reading the latest issue of *American Rifleman*, legs crossed, looking very comfortable in his old rayons.

"Do you know a guy named James Oates at NASA?" I asked.

He looked from his page to me.

"Why?"

"He's my English teacher's boyfriend."

"Well," he said with relish, "then she's got herself a prize-winning, long-haired commie freak."

I soon realized that I'd abandoned hope too soon! No way would Miss Surratt stay with some "commie freak," whatever that was. I'd wait until I was eighteen, go out to San Francisco, and ask Miss Surratt to marry me. Five years to wait. Not long. Simple as that. I felt confident, especially after Maude called to ask me over to help Miss Surratt pack for her trip. I figured to get her new address then.

When my mom dropped me off in front of the Cooling Pond Apartments, I found Miss Surratt's boxes lining the curb. She'd hitched a bright orange-and-white U-Haul to her blue VW and was loading. I scarcely recognized Miss Surratt, the way her breasts, now pendulous, swam freely in her white tee, how the black shades she wore made her eyes seem plucked out. Her feet were bare, and the hems of her tattered bellbottoms rasped on the sidewalk, even more grating than Mr. Doty's pronunciation of vagina.

From her right ear, and only from the right, through a gaping, red-sore puncture, dangled a large metal hoop. Inside the hoop was a symbol, like an upside-down 'Y' with the fork in the 'Y' divided. I could not help but stare in silence, even after Miss Surratt said, "It's nice for you to come and help!"

Maude set a box into the U-Haul, blew a rat of hair from her face, and caught me gawking at the horrible hoop hanging from Miss Surratt's right ear.

"It means 'Nuclear Disarmament,'" Maude whispered. "Like world peace or something, like when Hamlet says, 'To be or not to be,' I think she wants to *be*."

Back then I didn't care what it meant. I only saw how the earring threw everything off, how gravity seemed to seize the terrible thing, tug her ear closer to earth, burden everything beautiful, distant, and unattainable, like Miss Surratt had been.

After we loaded the U-Haul, Miss Surratt shook my hand. The mutinous glittering hoop of peace jounced against her neckline.

Maude said, "Good luck, Miss Surratt!"

I stood, silent.

After Miss Surratt drove off, Maude remained at my side, tired and frowning.

"You're pathetic," she said.

"So are you," I replied with the stock, unsupported eighth-grade comeback.

"Why didn't you just tell her you like her?" she said.

"Like her?"

"Yeah. Like her a *lot*."

How could I possibly explain what I'd lost when Miss Surratt had driven off?

I turned to Maude, said, "Do that thing with your eyes."

"Why?"

"Because I've never seen it."

"No."

"Come on."

And when Maude stuck her thumbs to her eyelids, when she rolled her eyeballs down in their sockets and they went entirely white, I leaned forward, closed my eyes, and kissed her lips, a kiss that cracked the silence that had surrounded me that summer. All I'd wanted to say to Miss Surratt drained out my ears . . . and in flowed the chatter of blackbirds on power lines, the jangle of return bottles as a kid dragged his Radio Flyer filled with them over a crack in the sidewalk, the hum of the pool filter, a breeze blubbering—the clangorous world split open and poured in. I waited for Maude to react to my kiss, my eyes shut tight, my world blank, a land of living blind. I waited to open my eyes, waited to see everything that sounded so fresh and new. But when Maude kissed me back and I opened my eyes, it was, like those in years to come, only another of many passing fascinations, while the world still trembled on the brink of extinction.

Prayer for Sitting Bull

David Eugene Brown, Jr.

O' Great White Father, the real one
Loved and beloved of the many buffalo,
Grant the wind and the planting moon,
The ease of the summer prairie
And the love song of the rustling grasses
To this, his spirit space,
Dreams left among ashen sons and daughters
Drifting helpless against mile after mile
Of rotting, rusting fence,
One sided cages stacked beyond the horizon of escape.
Longing without long existence
Or any existence at all
Dark children playing, rapidly fading,
Unremarked hopeless definition
"All Games Cancelled Today"
Read the sign
Atop the wall
In plain English.

The Leap

Bill Christophersen

The Saturday before our confirmation class
celebrated first communion, Pastor
took us on an outing to the Cloisters.
Late April. We climbed the looping paths
of Inwood Park to the heights; strolled
the abbey, the dark rooms hung with clay-
and wheat-colored tapestries portraying
medieval scenes, the temptations of Christ,
Abraham and Isaac, Daniel among the lions,
Ruth in the cornfield. Across the Hudson,
the palisades sported a crew cut of new
green. We shared crackers and fruit as Pastor
talked about faith, about what it means to
give your life to something greater than yourself.
On the way back down, Middleton and I
horsed around, fell behind. Seeing that the path
dipped in a long half hitch, we figured to take a
short cut down the mountain. It was steep, but
Middleton took off running. No punk, I
followed. Soon I couldn't stop. Had to
concentrate hard not to miss a step till the
incline gave onto the path. But where
was the path? Off to the side, Middleton
yelled something, ran into a tree. Directly
ahead was a drop, and beyond the drop,
treetops.

I

hit pavement about ten feet below.
Tumbled to the side in a shoulder roll that
knocked the wind out of me, then

footballed into the low railing along the
edge of the path, where the mountainside
continued. (Pastor speechless, the girls
gaping, goshing, tittering, saying how it
looked from where they were and did I think
I was Bat Man, Spider Man, Flash Gordon?) I
was a practiced hand at shrugging off spills and
keeping a poker face around girls and adults, but I
died and rose that day without spraining an ankle.

Unable to close my eyes at night, I tried to
put it all together. Was God, as Middleton thought,
an actual voice? ("Something like an intercom
told me, 'Run into that tree, knucklehead!'") If so,
why hadn't I heard it? Had I been slated for a more
cinematic rescue? I thought about Jonah, about the
men in the furnace, about Job with his lesions
and the but-me-no-buts voice in the whirlwind that
tells him where to get off before restoring his health.
Geez! Not only does the devil get to use him like a lab rat
God then chews him out for mouthing off! Was
this what I was dealing with? A whirlwind with
attitude? Or maybe just a whirlwind with a whirlwind's
sense of humor, removing the trees from my path when
I really could have used one, yet saving me anyway,
preventing me from breaking a leg, an arm, cracking my
skull, flying past that narrow asphalt end zone?
And what about faith? Did it routinely operate
through life-and-death pop quizzes? Had it ever
(or *just*?) moved a mountain? Could you
count on it? Develop it, like stomach muscles? Was it
a death pact? A lemming-like plunge? A
churchyard pose like the schoolyard poses kids
adopted? Or the real, game-changing deal-a

Bogart-like sangfroid that never backed down or
second-guessed itself, even while dancing on air?
I was no Bogie. But I had dodged a bullet. Though I
hadn't actually dodged, and felt more like the bullet.

Toward morning I awoke in a sweat. I dreamed I'd
taken a dare to leap from rooftop to rooftop but
slipped and fallen. In every window I passed on the
way down, I saw an apostle being whipped, burned,
beaten, crucified.
                              Sunday morning
we received the sacraments (the wafer dry
as Pastor had said it would be, the wine
a rush in the sinuses), then got our picture taken
with Pastor in front of the altar: the girls
gowned and permed, Middleton in a maroon-
and-brown-checked sports coat, me in a
charcoal suit, white shirt and alien eyes-
red dots where the flashbulb glinted off my glasses.

The Web

Michael J. Shepley

Intricate
well constructed
every invented thread
taut for more
than symbolic meaning
art formed
physical poem
of near perfect
geometric logic

A fisher's net
of concentric circles
somewhat squared
a kind of harp
waiting for the
first note of a
song of dinner

Hunger incarnate
inhabits its center
the creator focus
forever self-centered

like a poet

Ironically fated
to be devoured
by the myriad
of her own
starving offspring

Facts and Supplications

Curtis VanDonkelaar

Franklin, at the dining room table beside Lorraine,
tried to move the tablecloth and she reached across the
linen—he thought—to hold his hand. The folded cloth
lay diagonally across the hard wood. That was artsy to
Franklin. He would've liked the table either fully
covered by the cloth, which would have been normal,
or fully exposed, because the mahogany was
beautifully dark.

> Lorraine caught Franklin's hand and pushed
> his fingers flat to the table, so that he couldn't
> move them, or the cloth. Last week, she had
> accidentally gouged the table with a carving
> knife. She had to cover the scar so that
> Franklin wouldn't ever see. She knew this
> about him: things were better when he didn't
> know too much.

"The Earth's core moves faster than the crust," he said.
"I read that."

> The sort of thing he would say, Lorraine
> thought, just as the sort of thing a fly might
> do was to land on a windowpane and lick its
> shitty forearms, sit still right in the most visi-
> ble place, the most carefree spot, where she
> could smash it with her red-handled swatter.
> And she would, too, just as soon as that stu-
> pid meat touched glass.
> She frowned.
> "What was it yesterday?" she asked.
> "Something about daydreams and
> Alzheimer's?"

"Yes," he said.

> "The scientists think that daydreaming—" she went on, "—have I got this right? —that daydreaming works a space in your head, the same space where Alzheimer's happens. That daydreaming gives you one of those things, oh what's the word, a predisposition."

God, how Franklin hated that flyswatter, how Lorraine would lay it on the dining room table after use, not even wiping it clean. She could take a minute, he believed, to put it away, and not just lay about with death on her hands. He had loved her since the tenth grade, a thousand years ago, but every day of late had been to contract polio, over and over and over. He hoped that someday, they might like to be happy again, but he also liked to dream.

"Yes," he said. "I read that."

> "So." Lorraine traced her finger down the tablecloth. She could feel herself getting older. "Don't you wonder, maybe, how they make ships? How they bend the wood? Wouldn't you like to think about that, say, for half an hour? Or better yet, take an hour. I'll go to the store."

"You gotta dream," Franklin said, "in a dirty world.
And this one's filthy. Haha, big joke. Turns out,
dreams rot your brain."

> "No worse than your planet nonsense."
> Spinning hunk of rock, she thought. Melted rock, liquid, like mud. Crust on the outside, a slow-moving layer, a coat of papier-mâché. Lorraine had never played with mud as a child—who would want? —but she felt certain that Franklin had. He wasn't a bad husband, not really, but he wasn't a man at all. He was a

small boy, sitting in a patch of wet dirt, eating
mud like baker's chocolate, smiling and
smearing a cat's thick whiskers onto his face.
His mud was just dirt, but he ate nonetheless.
He'd eat until the world had nothing but
sand-baked glass for skin.
"Do you want a divorce?" he asked. "Because just say
the word."

"The word?" she said. "Divorce?"
Franklin had a suspicion that the problem was always
Lorraine. Lorraine slapping and pushing at him to think like a
dope, Lorraine with her mind a shut-up bodega, Lorraine who
never stopped to consider what any one thing meant. She was
swimming in all the wrongs between them, Lorraine who
balked, and poked, and froze, and who was also an impatient
lover.

He nodded. Then he cupped her hand in his own. "I
would never. Just so's you know."

"No," she said. "I wouldn't dream."

The Killing

Bruce Kirby

I missed my exit today
thinking of you

the way you were always unfolding
never unfolded

you were my nymphony
a harmony of desire and fire

but you opted for omitment
not commitment

a leap from love to leave

done playing
the cat gathers over the mouse

The Joy of Collecting

Jennifer Holden Ward

During my college years, my brother Mike, uncle Bo, and I tried to go around the world. Our goal: have a beer in every country. Or, at least, as many as we could manage on the July day we spent globetrotting at Disney's EPCOT Center.

Sometime after we had downed steins of dark beer in Germany and ordered Dos Equis in Mexico, the heavens opened and torrential rains began to fall. Adults ripped open packages of Mickey Mouse ponchos, children in strollers screamed as they became drenched, families dashed to find cover. International pavilions, which normally saw no traffic for their sleepy panoramic movies, were flooded with guests. Mike, Bo, and I took off on foot, abandoning our watered-down beers and soggy nachos. We opened the first door we came to, entering a dark hallway in a white building with no sign.

"Let's go this way," Bo said, motioning for Mike and me to follow him down the corridor.

"Where are we?" I asked.

We giggled as we walked along, water dripping from our clothing and leaving a path like breadcrumbs down the hallway. Then we heard voices — enthusiastic, Disney-like, Magical Day kinds of voices. As we rounded the corner and turned left, we saw the many people responsible for those voices sitting in a small auditorium.

A smiling man stood on stage wearing a blue vest and holding a microphone before three hundred mesmerized people. His voice was caffeinated with enthusiasm, but it wasn't his demeanor that held the audience spellbound. It was his words: "That's right, in just thirty minutes, in select locations around this park, we will release a limited number of what you've all been waiting for!"

Three hundred people maniacally clapped their hands, turning to their neighbors to exchange looks of glee. Mike, Bo, and I just looked at each other and laughed — the feeling in this place was contagious. What was this man about to release that would make these people so happy? One had only to look closer (maybe to observe their attire) and the answer would be obvious. Every single person in that room less Mike, Bo, and me, wore a lanyard or a vest crammed with shiny little pins. We had stumbled upon a Disney Underground – the world of Disney pin collecting.

"Pin Collectors, we know this is what you've been waiting for, and you're about to get it!!!" Crazy applause for the man on stage.

"We are handing out a map of locations where you can find this gem – the limited edition Flubber pin!" Audience members jumped from their seats and bounced in place, cheering. They hugged each other and tittered with excitement. Mike and Bo joined in, clapping, posing for pictures with the mob behind them, trying to push their way to the front of the crowd to be part of the hype. It was hard not to get caught up.

Nor was it easy to avoid the stampede when the man on stage yelled, "Ready! Set! Go!"

Off went three hundred pin collectors down the hall, out the door, lanyards blowing in the wind, jogging through the rain over footbridges, through gardens, until, after ten minutes of hunting, they reached their Mecca – a Flubber pin-filled, bona fide Disney Pin Collectors kiosk. Mike, Bo, and I were right there with them. We watched the collectors line up. They bonded over their common interest, showing off their rarest pieces, trading pins with total strangers as they stood waiting for their shot at acquiring Flubber.

We had our chance to buy Flubber that day, but we did not purchase pins. Amid all the excitement, we did not begin sporting lanyards or donning vests. The rain stopped falling, and the pin collectors dispersed to enjoy the rest of the day in the park. And I was left with one sobering thought: I am a collector of nothing.

I suppose you could say I once tried my hand at this collecting thing. I failed. When I was seven years old, I declared myself a sticker collector, mostly because someone gave me a book called "My Sticker Collection." I would add a glittery star or a red heart sticker every once in a while, but the majority of the time I'd forget about it and then, feeling guilty about being a slacker, cram to add a bunch of stickers all at once.

Not much has changed. As an adult, I do not grow giddy to add a new snow baby to a curio cabinet. I do not yearn to find the Alaska coin to complete a state quarter collection. And I do not lose sleep at night perusing eBay for a still-in-the-box Cabbage Patch Kid. My garden is not home to a collect-them-all set of gnomes. I go to jewelry parties where women gush over charm bracelets, chattering about which silver dangly thingy to add to their wrists next, and I buy nothing. I have tried keeping diaries or travel journals, but I fail to write in them for weeks, months, even years at a time. It seems I cannot even collect my thoughts.

You would think the urge to collect would have been passed down like heirloom china from mother to daughter; my mother is an avid collector of things – the definition of "things" depending on the time period. In the 1990s, she collected Longaberger baskets by the carload. She had so many baskets that she bought an eyesore called a basket tree, a tall wrought iron rod with short hooks stemming off every side. She would hang the baskets, even mini ones with no function, from the tree's "branches" and declare that even though the baskets didn't look particularly useful while hanging on a tree, they were there to look pretty. Thereby becoming purposeful simply by hanging. The basket fad ended, and my mother sold many in her collection. Ask her why she ever began collecting them and she'll claim she was sucked into it by friends and family who sold and collected them. Then she'll probably raise her hand as she swears: "I am no longer part of the cult."

Yet since the millennium, my mother has gone through periods of collecting lightweight sweat suits, Vera Bradley bags, raincoats, Mickey Mouse imprinted soap, and down-filled Pottery Barn furniture. For Christmas last year, she got a Pandora bracelet and plans to collect beads symbolizing each of her five grand-children. But those of us who know her doubt her ability to stop once she hits the mark. She will need another fix.

My mother comes by collecting honestly; her own mother collected Lladro porcelain dolls. "When I was eight, my mother told me I needed to have a collection and told me it should be dolls," my mother says. "Then she took me to the store and told me to pick out a doll to get for Christmas – one that I had to put on a shelf." Doll-collecting commenced. And, I suppose, in an effort to not become like her own mother, my mother never made me start a collection of my own.

Without understanding where the urge to collect comes from, I can't be certain whether or not I should mourn the collecting gene's omission from my DNA, celebrate, or just blame my mother. How in the world did collecting begin, and why do people have these impulses? I set out on a quest and began, well, collecting information.

History is full of collectors. William Randolph Hearst collected art. Thomas Jefferson collected books. Henry VIII collected wives. But to determine the true origin of collecting, I turned to Russell Belk, author of *Collecting in a Consumer Society*, professor of marketing at York University, and fellow collector of nothing. According to Belk, collectors date back to the fourth century B.C. in Ancient Greece where, due to new wealth under Alexander the Great, Greeks collected secular paintings, statues, Oriental carpets, wall hangings, and furniture. Collecting caught on in Ancient Rome too – first with the rulers and then with private collectors, like Lucius Cornelius Sulla, a Roman general and politician who later became the first great private collector. By the beginning of the Roman Empire, everyone who could manage to collect was doing so. "Once the Romans discovered Greek artifacts, there was a surge in collecting simply because there were interesting things to collect," Belk says. Dealers opened in Rome selling art, books, and jewelry. Even people who could not afford original artwork or tapestries collected coins, fossils, and oddities like insects trapped in amber.

Collecting began in the U.S. when settlers accumulated Indian arrowheads and hunting trophies. Initially, most collecting here was limited to clergymen or to the wealthy. In the twentieth century, thanks to mass production, Americans began collecting more, and the items they collected varied from comic books to cigar bands to, well, Disney pins. "It's been estimated that one-third of North Americans collect," Belk says.

Today, people collect anything from coat hangers to X-rays to airsickness bags. Perhaps the oddest collection belongs to Graham Barker, a self-described "slightly larger than average male" resident of Perth, Australia, who collects his "navel fluff" or belly button lint. According to his website, Barker, who holds the Guinness World Record for navel lint, deems his collection unique and rare and his navel lint in mint condition. If asked why he collects it, Barker responds, "Why not?" Mason jars of belly button lint as home décor. Why not, indeed.

Perhaps a collector's urge goes back to our hunter and gatherer days. We stockpile things in case of hard times. Or maybe some collectors just crave the hunt and get an adrenaline rush from finding something of value. Belk insists some collect because the collection is something bigger than the self, and collectors think they're contributing to art, history, and science. Some, like my mother, claim collecting is a learned behavior. Perhaps some collect just as a hobby and a way to pass the time. Like my brothers, whom I remember amassing baseball cards by the hundreds. On Saturday mornings in Sports Card Heroes, a small store off Main Street in Laurel, Maryland, my brothers would buy packs of sports cards, tear them open, and cast away the stale bubblegum. Then they would discern whether or not they had a valuable card in their stack.

On one visit, I decided to buy a pack of hockey cards out of sheer boredom. My brothers had been buying packs of these cards for weeks hoping to find the Eric Lindros rookie card.

I ripped open the pack and began to flip through the cards. I read the names until I came to Eric Lindros.

"This one?" I asked Mike. "Is this the guy?"

Mike looked down at my cards and yelled, "Yes, that's it! I can't believe *you* found it!"

Me.

The one who collects nothing.

Mike showed me how to buy a thick glass case for the card so it could be displayed without risking it being mishandled and therefore devalued. I doubt the card is worth much these days, which is lucky since I don't have a clue where it is. Surely if I were a collector, I would be able to locate my collection.

Plus, one hockey card does not a collection make. It's about having a set, not a pile but rather select variations of an object. Quality over quantity. "It's almost like getting a new family member," Belk says of a collector adding a piece. The collector defines boundaries for the collection and then embarks on a journey to find the objects. A collector thinks: "This is a mission. Now we know where to stop on vacation and people know what to buy us as gifts," Belk says. Yet by creating a cadre of specific goods, the collector removes the item's functional capacity to add it to her collection. In other words, the collected items are rendered useless – they just sit there collecting dust.

Consider an antique book collector. "Rather than 'spoil' a book from the collection, they buy a new copy of the book when they want to read it," Belk says. So the book collector has two collections: one for show and one for use.

Take Anniken Davenport, an attorney from Pennsylvania who collects the past. It doesn't matter whose past it is, she just likes to preserve it. She hates the idea that people allow the material proof of their family's heritage to disappear by selling heirlooms, so she purchases antiques online. She claims her collecting habit started innocently enough when she helped her son sell things on eBay. She began logging on to make her own purchases.

Davenport began with Norwegian silver, a nod to her homeland. Then she collected sets of vases and figurines, until she began an obsession with fine linen tablecloths. "The older, the better," she says about the linens. She preferred that they be in mint condition, unused. And she liked finding ones with elaborate scenes like The Last Supper or nymphs frolicking in fountains or even battle tableaus.

To date, Davenport has more than three hundred tablecloths (she owns one table), two hundred napkins, and cabinets full of knitting yarn – all proof, she thinks, that she has a compulsion with collecting. "I think the obsession has to do with reaching back to a world of craftsmanship and quality that is long gone," she says. "You can't get anything of quality or value at Wal-Mart, and I deplore the idea that the accoutrements of civilization are gone. I refuse to live in such a world." So instead she fills her house with things from a world past.

Davenport also collects hardback books, sterling silver spoons, and enamel spoons, and she crams them into her 1,200-square-foot townhouse, which is decorated in what she calls "Victorian Clutter" style. Collectors like Davenport cannot possibly use everything they accumulate, no matter if they collect useful goods or trinkets.

Claiming an addiction as Davenport does is a way for the collector to humorously free herself from responsibility for her

addiction, Belk says. But Belk, who doesn't categorize collect-
ing as either good or bad, says the hobby offers some benefits,
including social pleasure from interacting with other collectors
(consider the pin collectors bonding in the rain), the thrill of
participating in a competitive activity, and what he calls "small
world control." The collector, who cannot control everything
in the world around her, "can manage and rule the small world
that she created with a collection," Belk says. For some, it is a
form of self-expression that fosters identity; for others, it is a
way to channel energy, time, and money. Studying collecting
doesn't seem to be an exact science. But most researchers agree
that collecting, as long as it doesn't cross that nasty line and
become hoarding, is a healthy hobby that brings pleasure.

On a recent winter morning, I stood in *Cute Souvenirs* on
the corner of Forty-Second Street and Fifth Avenue in New
York City, looking for a token to take home to Baltimore. The
store was taller than it was wide, and the owners had taken
advantage of the high ceilings to display their stock. Burly
salesmen, black hair slicked back, manned the store's perimeter.
They held long rods with hooks on the end ready to pull down
from the high shelves anything a patron desired.

"What do you want to see? What can I get for you?" they
would ask, tilting and ducking their heads up and down,
attempting to make eye contact with shoppers as they walked
past. Their unsolicited help was occasionally met with a tight
smile, but more often ignored.

I walked through the store, avoiding eye contact, looking
at the merchandise. I ran my fingers along silver plates
engraved with the Statue of Liberty. I eyed snow globes of
Central Park. I grew dizzy counting "I heart NY" T-shirts. The
store offered all the usual fare: refrigerator magnets, bottle
openers, coffee mugs in two sizes, ashtrays, spoon rests,
miniature license plates, and bobblehead dolls of President
Barack Obama.

As I stood there, I thought about my quest. To someone out there, the sight of that Ellis Island ashtray is a welcome one and maybe a defining moment for her collection. To someone out there, no matter her reasons, seeing that personalized New York thimble makes her day. To someone out there, finding that shiny silver spoon is like Gollum seizing his ring. The item, itself, is precious. That someone is not me.

Mr. Dow's Story

Jill Birdsall

It came as no surprise when Mr. Dow died. When we were dating and he wanted sex, he was dying. After we married he wanted to go to his mother's instead of mine for holiday, dying. I'm going to die, he told me when I wanted him to paint the kitchen. His grandfather and father died young so he was sure he would follow suit. Forty was the magic age. By forty he would be dead.

I imagined his death, considered the ways: His recliner collapsed under him; it swallowed him up. He ate himself to death – six hotdogs with the works followed by chocolate cheesecake. Or maybe he'd die of King Tut's curse: while shaving cut a mosquito bite on his face, suffer infection, erysipelas, ending in blood poisoning and pneumonia.

He was dying, he told me. "Now scratch my back," he said, lifting his shirt behind him. Or, "Scratch my head." He was going bald and thought the stimulation to his scalp would bring back his hair.

When he celebrated forty, "You were wrong!" I said. "You lived."

I didn't sound happy, he said.

"You sound disappointed!" were his exact words.

"You're a liar," I told him. "All that time lying."

During my marriage to Mr. Dow I developed rheumatoid arthritis. The chronic pain made me cranky. I had trouble getting out of bed. I visited specialists and tried an exhaustive list of treatments – analgesics, anti-inflammatories, corticosteroids. I tried physical therapy, even joint replacement. Nothing helped.

Mr. Dow kept it up.

"You'll be the death of me," he said.

He may have gotten beyond the heart failure that killed his ancestors. It was me now. I asked him to carry the garbage can to the road. I was working him to death. When I salted his ham, "You're trying to kill me." He recited a litany of lines and every one pointed a finger at me.

By his fiftieth birthday, I planned his wake. It would be one day. Closed casket. The funeral home in town would be easiest. His family hated photos, mine expected them. An easel in each corner of the room, the best photo framed on top of the casket. I pulled the best from our albums, closeups of his face, his jawline and amazing chin. I locked these in a hidden desk drawer, afraid if I looked too closely or too often, they would no longer be what I thought they were. When I washed our dishes I daydreamed the flowers I'd lay across his coffin – all white, a mix of roses and hydrangea. And while he blew out the fifty candles on his birthday cake, I thought of the candle I'd bring to the funeral home, sweet-violet, because, in my opinion, all funeral homes emit a horrid laboratory odor.

"Why are you hunching?"

He moved like he had arthritis but I was the one who had that. He asked me to read things to him. He could no longer see, he said. I had to open jars and bottles. He had no strength, he told me. I did my best to hold his jacket while he got into it because he said his shoulders had stopped rotating.

"See a doctor," I told him. "I'll make an appointment for you."

I thought maybe he would see someone. Maybe he'd do it because I wanted him to, and because he wanted to stay with me; he didn't want to die and leave me like he said. But as quickly as I thought it, I knew better.

"Over my dead body," he said.

The church service took no time to plan. He wasn't a churchgoer so it was a series of random picks. He didn't have favorite readings or songs. What he'd want, I knew, was to get in and out. He wasn't one to waste time. No burial. No cemetery plot. Cremation. He didn't like to waste anything. But things began to run out on their own. Things were used up. I couldn't hear him anymore, could no longer reach my arm to scratch his back. Mr. Dow's hair was gone. His teeth fell out. The more that left us, the quieter we were.

Except every so often, "You made me this way," he said.

"You made me this way," I said back at him.

Mr. Dow was eighty when he died, twice as old as he planned. He died in his sleep.

I watched his cremation through a window. I didn't press the button or anything, but I had to watch or I'd think it hadn't happened. I saw them check him for a pacemaker, glasses or any jewelry. Once the incinerator was preheated a mechanized door opened. They sent him inside in a box and then they sealed the door. They aimed the flame at his torso. His skin split, muscles charred. His bones were last to go. It's over when they crumble. It took two hours.

They gave me six pounds of ash. I keep these in a tumbler next to my bed. His ashes are gray like his hair but not soft like I thought ashes should be. They're like gravel. In my sleep, I touch them to be sure he's there. I dip a finger in then rub it on my cheek like he's just touched me. Next day I look like I've been through a fire. I carry his ashes to the kitchen with me each morning.

It takes a long time to learn certain things. It took a long time for me to learn that Mr. Dow and I were a perfect pair. When two things don't go together, put them together and see what happens. Like the morning I dropped a teaspoon full of Mr. Dow in boiling water. Like medicine, I drank it down.

Three Things I Used to Know

Midge Raymond

It starts with the staring. I always think I have spinach in my teeth, or toilet paper stuck to my heel—then they approach me. It happened in L.A. a couple of months ago, and it's happened once here in Ashland, too, in the court-yard outside the Elizabethan theatre. This time, it happens on the street—Gage has just arrived, and we're walking downtown for lunch when I notice her: a woman snatching quick glances in our direction, as if trying to be subtle, before finally sidling up to us and waiting for a pause in our conversation.

"Excuse me," the woman says, with a quick glance at Gage before turning her attention back to me. "I'm a huge fan. Would you mind?" She holds out a blank envelope. I can tell there's a card inside and wonder briefly who it's for and whether she'll buy a new one if I mar this one with my autograph.

I smile and shake my head. "I'm sorry." I put my hand on her arm to soften what I'm about to say. "I don't give auto-graphs."

"Oh." She looks confused, embarrassed.

"It's just as a rule. I'm sorry." I continue to smile as warmly as I can, then turn back to Gage, whose lips are pressed together. As we cross the street, a breeze brings cool air from the mountains, which rise up on both sides of the valley into a bright, marbled sky. I pull open the door of a café, and Gage follows me inside, looking bemused.

"Did that ever happen back in college?" I ask. "People mistaking me for someone famous?"

"Never," he says with a laugh. "Who do they think you are, anyway?"

It's been years since I've heard the sound of his laugh. "No idea," I say. It's always both a surprise and a thrill to be mistaken for a celebrity; I've only ever been a wife and a mother and a teacher. Since moving to Ashland, I've begun to call myself an artist, but that identity is only about a month old and doesn't seem real yet. And none of it would sound very exciting if I admitted it to strangers who think they've had a celebrity sighting.

"That's why I don't sign my name," I tell Gage. "So I can let them have their fantasy."

"And so you can have yours," he says.

At the café counter, I watch Gage study the menu. We haven't shared a meal together in a decade, but he doesn't surprise me; he orders lentil soup and a tofu wrap, all vegan. The last time I saw him had been at our ten-year college reunion—we'd both skipped the twentieth—and he looks exactly the same: shaggy hair, stubble on his jaw, trim build, as if he hadn't aged a day.

We take a table near the window, looking out over Main Street. From across the table, he looks at me and says, "Christine Lahti."

"What?"

"That's who you might look like, back in her *Chicago Hope* days. Or maybe that skinny blonde from *Lost*, the one who was Hugo's soul mate from the mental hospital."

"You're dating yourself, Gage." I can see what he means, though: the light hair, a just-above-average prettiness, a thin fortysomething look. "I always assume they take me for Emma Stone," I joke.

He grins, then turns his eyes toward the window. A trio of dreadlocked men with a dog walk past, all dressed in fatigues, loaded down with rucksacks, facial hair to mid-chest. They remind me of a younger Gage, and I wonder whether he's thinking the same thing when he exchanges a nod with them as they pass the café.

Then he turns back to me. "The problem is, you're out there ruining reputations," he says. "Every time you refuse to give an autograph, someone goes away thinking that some innocent celebrity is a rude bitch who doesn't appreciate her fans."

"What am I supposed to sign," I ask, "if I don't know who they think I am?"

"Just scribble down something illegible," he says. "Then everybody's happy."

It's how I've remembered him—the peacemaker.

"So how's the hubby?"

"He's great," I say. "Looking forward to seeing you."

I'm sure Gage can hear the lie in my voice, but he doesn't say anything. *I didn't know you were still in touch with him,* Tod had said last week, when I told him Gage was spending the night with us on his way to Portland. When I asked Tod why he'd assumed that, he said, *You two are just so different.* What he really meant, I think, is that he and Gage are different—that he can't understand how I could be married to him and still find anything in common with Gage.

"Now I feel guilty," I say, "for tarnishing all these celebrity reputations."

"You were always like that," Gage says. "Always feeling guilty about one thing or another."

And I feel guilty even now, sitting here across from him. On the surface, this is just an innocent lunch, a visit between friends—but deep down I'm having the same thoughts I've had about him for years, stirring again like sediment at the bottom of a still pond suddenly rustled to the surface, clouding everything.

A server brings our lunch, and I'm relieved to turn away from Gage's eyes. I reach over to the next table for a salt shaker.

After a spoonful of soup, he says, "I was surprised to hear that you and Tod were retiring so early."

"It still surprises me sometimes, too."

"So whose idea was it, anyway?"

"Retirement, his. Moving here, mine."

"Are you happy about it?"

"Of course."

"Didn't you like teaching?"

I pick up my fork. I'd ordered an eggplant panini, and the olive oil has soaked through the bread, causing the sandwich to fall apart in my hands. "I loved teaching art," I say, "but I also wanted to be *making* art. With Katy, summers always filled up so quickly, I never got any of my own work done."

"And now I've shown up," he says, "taking you away from your studio time."

"I'm glad you're here," I say.

Gage lives in New York, in the same rent-controlled Lower East Side studio he's had for decades. He'd sent photos once, when I asked—a dim little place, with only two windows, a bathtub in the kitchen—but he said it was perfect, that all he ever needed was a place to crash. Since college, he's lived a life that I've always secretly envied; he writes songs and plays guitar and bartends at various clubs and hotels. He flew to San Francisco last week for a folk-music gig and is now on his way to Portland for a poetry festival. He didn't indicate how long he'd stay, and I didn't ask, just told him that my daughter's room was all his for as long as he wanted it.

"I can't wait to show you my studio," I tell him. "We converted the garage."

"I'd love to see some of your work."

"Well, I'm just getting started. The place is still a bit of a mess." Tod has left most of the unpacking to me while he goes to the university library to write. I try not to meet Gage's eye as I think about the way I've been unpacking, the almost subconscious way I've divided up Tod's and my things—his books on one shelf, mine on another; his bachelor-party barware in one cupboard, my mother's sherry glasses in another. I've already begun drawing lines between what's his and what's mine.

I see that Gage is watching me and I quickly glance away. "I'm in the mood for dessert, aren't you?" Before he can answer, I head for the counter, where I pretend to examine the home-made pies.

Gage and I met in a poetry class, and when I look back, I think it must have been the poetry, the reading and interpreting of it in his dorm room, on Boston Common, in smoky cafés, that created the intimacy that sprouted between us. I was already dating Tod, across the river at M.I.T., but Gage and I became close, nearly inseparable. Though Gage and I were only friends (as I told Tod) and though I was in love with Tod (as I told Gage), I always felt as if I were cheating on one with the other.

Gage was a year younger than Tod and me, and late one warm spring night—or probably it was early morning—just before the end of my junior year and Gage's sophomore year, he and I were sprawled on a couch in the common room of his dorm, having just finished whatever beer was still in his fridge, or whatever pot was still in the baggie in his desk. I had my head on his shoulder when he said, his mouth close to my ear, *I love you, you know.* I'd murmured drowsily, *Love you back,* but he had paused, then clarified: *No, I mean I really love you.*

Gage's revelation, combined with whatever I was under the influence of that night, left me temporarily stunned. My first thought was of Tod, whom I'd been dating for more than a year by then—a man so much more my type than Gage, or so I thought. The two of them have always been so different—Gage, like a transplant from another century, loved the simple things: guitar music; reading poetry, writing it. Tod was twenty-first century all the way: precise, single-minded, literal. He always knew exactly what he wanted—whenever Tod put his mind to something, he excelled, and back then his priority was to make me happy. He went out of his way to know everything about what I liked, even if he himself didn't care for spa weekends or wine tastings. He planned trips and gifts with meticulous detail, and the attention was intoxicating. And as much as I enjoyed being with Gage, with scruffy, sloppy, free-spirited Gage, the one with whom I shared daydreams and drugs, he wasn't a guy I could imagine settling down with.

Until that night, as we sat there together on the couch, as I straightened up to look at him. I wondered for a moment whether I needed to be more open-minded, whether my own life needed to be less practical, less polished. I was struggling to form a response to him in my mind when Gage continued talking, telling me he was leaving, going to Paris for his junior year, heading over that summer to travel—the plans were all in place, and he'd done it all without telling me because he knew I was committed to Tod and that it would be easier for him if he went away.

I didn't know what to say—so I said nothing, and he left for Paris. And things played out as I'd expected all along: by the end of our senior year, Tod and I were engaged, and Gage had a French girlfriend. Gage did not come to our wedding, and he and I lost touch until our tenth reunion. I'd gone to Boston by myself, leaving Tod at home with Katy; Gage, perpetually single, came alone, too. We went to every event together: the alumni mixers and the after-parties, the Red Sox game and the pub crawl. On our last night in Boston, as we walked back to the hotel, both of us a little drunk, he said, *Nothing's changed. I thought I'd feel differently about you. But I feel exactly the same.* He'd kissed me then, a long, feverish kiss that erased the last ten years and put us back on that couch in his dorm all those years ago—and then he pulled away and walked down the hall to his room. I lay awake for a long time that night, wanting to go to him, forcing myself to think of my family, of my daughter. I stayed where I was.

Under the circumstances, I shouldn't have stayed in touch with Gage at all, but email has made it easy, and his messages have become sporadic but necessary lifelines. I've clung to them the way I cling to the idea of letting people believe I'm someone famous.

But of course such thoughts are absurd for a middle-aged empty nester, and since the reunion I've tried to suppress them. On the day I'd returned, the feel of Gage's lips still numbing my own, Tod had asked vaguely how the reunion had been, and I'd told him it was fine. After dinner, as we loaded the dishwasher, he said, in a teasing voice, *So did you run into any old boyfriends?*

I felt my cheeks burn as I said, *Of course not. Besides, in college there wasn't anyone but you.*

Didn't you have some friend you hung around with all the time? I always thought he had a thing for you.

I poured the last of the wine into my glass and paused before saying, *Gage was there.* I felt the need to be at least semi-honest. *We exchanged email addresses, but that was about it.*

That's good.

Still holding my wine, I put my arms around Tod, watching the wine slosh in the glass. *There are three things I know,* I told him. *I love you. I love Katy. And this is exactly where I want to be.*

I knew it was myself I was trying to convince, and I embraced him so he couldn't see my face. Later, when we went up to bed, I found myself trying to remember when all three of those things had been true at once—and they had been true, for many years—and what it had felt like when they were.

After lunch, as Gage and I walk back to the house, I feel relieved that he'd never visited when Tod and I lived in Silicon Valley, where everything is oversized. Our new house is a small craftsman with two bedrooms, plus an office for Tod. Accustomed to having a three-car garage, Tod now has to park his BMW in a short driveway, where it barely fits. When Gage arrived earlier, he'd parked his old Toyota there, not realizing that the detached garage is my studio, that he'd taken Tod's spot.

Inside, Gage's bag and guitar case are still on the floor in the kitchen, where we'd left them earlier. I show him to Katy's room, and he looks around, taking in the swimming trophies, the posters of Dara Torres and Natalie Coughlin.

He picks up a gold swimming medal, holding it by its patriotic red, white, and blue ribbon. "Remember," he asks, grinning, "when we used to steal stuff from each other?"

He knows I'd never forget. It was a running joke of ours in college, though I'm not sure which one of us did it first. We spent so much time in each other's dorm rooms, we began to sneak things out, then wait for the other to catch on. Eventually, if he didn't notice I'd stolen a shirt, I'd wear it to a class we had together. If I didn't detect filched jewelry, Gage would wear it when he met me at out at a bar. I still remember the sight of him wearing one of my necklaces, a delicate gold chain nestled into the concave spot right below his Adam's apple.

"You'd have to take that down to L.A. if you want Katy to notice it," I say. "We dropped her off at USC a couple of months ago."

He smiles and returns the medal to the dresser. "Wish I could've met her."

"Maybe next time," I say.

"What's she like?"

"She's a good kid."

"What's she studying?"

"Other than her boyfriend? We don't know yet."

This has been one of the few things Tod and I have agreed on lately; we both hoped, since she'd spent all her life in California, that Katy would go to college on the east coast. She showed no interest because, as we found out later, her boyfriend had also been accepted to USC—they'd planned all along to stay together.

I wanted to tell her, *Don't do it; you're too young!* But I knew that she would say, *You married Dad right out of college, didn't you? That worked out, didn't it?* And there was no way I could tell her that it hadn't.

My own parents will be married fifty years next summer, the same year Tod and I celebrate our twentieth. My brother and sister and I have been talking about doing something special for them—Sabrina says that gold is the traditional gift for a fiftieth anniversary, but Peter wants to give them an experience, like a trip, a vacation they'd never plan on their own. I've let them argue it out while I contemplate my own anniversary. Tod and I haven't talked about it, and I wonder if he even counts the years anymore.

I can't help but worry that Katy will end up like me. That one day she'll be as many years into her marriage as I am into mine, wondering how she'll get through the rest of it without anything being truly wrong but without everything being truly right—wondering and perhaps even imagining what could've been and isn't.

Gage is taking his guitar out of its case, and I watch him set it on the bed. "Why don't we go open some wine," I say, and he picks up the guitar and follows me downstairs.

We're halfway through the bottle when Tod comes home. He shakes hands with Gage but declines our offer of wine and starts a pot of coffee. "I thought we'd walk into town for dinner," I say. "Where do you want to eat?"

"I'm writing tonight," Tod says.

"You're not going to join us?"

I don't know why I'm surprised; Tod's never been very social. He'd skipped out on most of his own holiday parties at work, and I always have to drag him to other couples' homes for dinner. I finally began to go without him, making up a sudden illness for Tod, a sudden work emergency. *Tod sends his best,* I'd say. *He wishes he could be here.* And eventually, when I began to accept invitations without Tod—when I said, *Tod can't make it, but I'd love to come*—I would get uninvited, rescheduled for *a time when Tod can join us.* It was as if Tod's absence sent everyone's thoughts to unwanted places, as if they imagined Tod dead, or having left me; as if they imagined it happening to them. Now I'm finding that it's a relief to be new in town, to not know anyone, to have no invitations to skirt around or decline.

I don't know what to say to Tod, and in the silence that follows, Gage asks him, "So, what are you working on?"

"A novel."

"What's it about?"

"Too early to talk about it."

"You can tell him a *little* about it," I say, and turn to Gage. "It's a thriller. Set in Silicon Valley, all about a new software virus that can—"

"Jackie, I meant it. I'm not ready to talk about it."

I look at him. "You've told me about it. I just thought—"

"It's a work in progress," he interrupts. "That's all."

"We writers are peculiar that way," Gage says. "Don't sweat it."

Tod's coffee hasn't finished brewing, but he fills a travel mug anyway. "Back to work," he says.

"Are you sure you don't want something to eat, at least?" I motion toward the food I've brought out: hummus and pita, spiced nuts and olives.

"No, I should get going," he says as he leaves the kitchen. "I need to think."

It has an ominous ring to it, like the phrase *we need to talk.* I can hear him packing his laptop in the other room, and when he passes through the kitchen again, I excuse myself and walk him to the door.

"Why are you being so rude?" I ask.

"I'm not being rude. I need to work."

"It's not *work*, Tod. You're retired, remember? You're supposed to be relaxing."

"I want to get this book done. You know that."

"What did they teach you at that writing retreat, anyway? How to Ignore Your Family 101? You've been weird ever since you got back."

"It's got nothing to do with the retreat." He glances in the direction of the kitchen. "Have a nice dinner. I'll be back late." And he leaves.

I return to the kitchen, and it's clear that Gage has overheard everything. "Sorry about that," I say.

He refills our glasses. "So where's this studio of yours?"

In the last of the day's light, we take our glasses outside, across the driveway to the garage. "It's a work in progress," I warn him as I open the garage door with the remote. The thin, goldish light fills the studio, highlighting the dust, the fact that I've hardly done any sculpting since I've been here. It's so badly organized: the kiln, the pottery wheel, a workbench, a large butcher block—all had been haphazardly unloaded while I was with the movers in the house.

Gage walks over to the table where I'm keeping several half-finished projects—a vase; a statue of a swimmer resembling Katy, my model; a mask for another piece I'd begun just before we started packing the old house.

He puts down his wine and picks up the mask, lightly touching its features with fingers callused from the guitar. I watch his hands move across the face.

"Tod doesn't like my being here," he says, then looks up at me. "Did you ever say anything about us?"

"There was nothing to tell him," I say, then add, "He's like that all the time. Still a workaholic."

"I keep wondering why you had to move," he says. "It makes sense that you want to get back to your art, but why leave your home? Do you even know anyone here?"

I shake my head. "I haven't really met anyone yet, but we're not too far from Woodside—less than a day's drive. We'll go back. Friends will visit."

"People always say that, but they never do."

"You're here, aren't you?"

"But you won't see me for another ten years."

"I hope that's not true."

As if to change the subject, he holds up the mask. "This face reminds me of yours."

I smile. "That's because it is. After Katy left, I didn't have a model, so I used my own face. Made a mold and everything. It needs work."

"Why?" he asks. "It's beautiful."

I wonder whether it's really my face he finds beautiful, or whether I've in some way made the mask look like a better version of me. That's the thing about art that I love, that I've missed—not only creating things but recreating them, just as you wish they actually were. As if I could turn myself into that celebrity everyone thinks they recognize on the street.

"It's not too bad," I say. "I'm going to rework it later."

"No, don't." He holds it up against the fading light, creating a silhouette. "Leave it exactly as it is."

After dinner, after another bottle of wine, Gage and I begin the walk back home. I want the evening to last—and I can't help glancing at passing cars, wondering if one of them might be Tod's—so I take Gage's hand and lead him into the park. It's dark and moonless, so we go only as far as the duck pond. We sit on a bench close enough to a lamp that we can still see each other but not so close that we're in a spotlight.

I don't let go of his hand, and I'm encouraged that he's okay with this. Gage, while not a monk by any means, hasn't had a serious girlfriend that I'm aware of—even the French girl hadn't lasted long—and over the years I've quit asking.

I imagine that at some point he decided that his bachelor life—the life that allows him to travel, to write and play music, to work irregularly, if at all—suits him well. I also imagine, perhaps too hopefully, that I remain part of the reason he's still single.

I squeeze his hand and rest my head against his shoulder. "This is nice," I say, and he murmurs agreement. It's a perfect autumn evening—cool but not cold, breezy but not windy—and just chilly enough that I have an excuse to inch closer to Gage.

"Jackie," he begins.

I lift my head. I know what he is about to say, and this time I want to be the one to say it first. I release his hand and reach up to touch his face. "I'm sorry I've waited so long," I say. Then I lean in close and kiss him.

I feel a split-second response, an echo of the hunger I felt in that kiss ten years ago—and then he's pulling back.

"Jackie," he says again. "I have to tell you something."

"What is it?" I run my finger down his throat, to that silky little hollow just below his Adam's apple.

"There's someone in my life now," he says.

Now it's my turn to pull back. "A woman?"

He laughs, and I'm glad it's too dark for him to see the color I feel rising in my cheeks. "Of course," he says. "You don't have to sound so shocked."

"I'm not, it's just—I mean, why didn't you mention her? You never said a word." I move slightly away from him. "And why didn't she come with you?"

He shifts a little on the bench, as if to give himself more distance. "She's working."

"Oh. What does she do?"

"She runs a women's clinic in the Bronx," he says. "She's about to take maternity leave, so she's been busy. A lot of loose ends to tie up."

"She's—having a baby?"

"Yes," he says. "We are."

"I'm—well, that's great. Wow. Big news."

He puts a hand on my knee, a pity gesture that makes me jerk my leg away. "I know. We're really excited."

"Why didn't you say anything?"

He shrugs. "You never ask."

I feel like diving into the duck pond, never coming up. "I shouldn't have—" I can't find a way to finish. "I didn't know—"

"It's okay." He lets out a little sigh, and when I look at him I can see his wistful smile in the dark. "I guess this makes us even, right?"

"I think I'm just reacting to—to something else. Something between Tod and me."

"What is it?"

I stare straight ahead, at the gently ripping water in the pond. "I think Tod's cheating on me."

"What?" I'm oddly comforted by the disbelief in his voice.

"Maybe it's over now. But I'm pretty sure he was. Last year, after he went to this writing retreat, he came back different. And then all of a sudden he was ready to retire. I've kept an eye out, checked his email, his phone. But there's nothing."

"Then you don't know for sure."

"I'm pretty sure." I'd never asked, mostly because I knew Tod couldn't lie, and I'm not sure whether I want my suspicions confirmed. "I just don't know what to do."

"Sounds like you already decided. You left your whole life and moved here with a man who's cheating on you."

"Woodside was never really *my* life to begin with," I say. "It wasn't where I chose to be. His work kept us there."

"What *is* your life, then?" he says. "If it's not the past twenty years, then what is it?"

I look at him and realize what I hadn't before, that there was a fourth thing I used to know, something I thought might still be true. Yet Gage is looking at me now with an expression

I'd refused to notice earlier, a serene but empty gaze that tells me he moved on long ago.

"I don't know," I say. "I guess I really have no idea."

The next morning, I get up early, with plans of walking downtown for cinnamon buns at the bakery. But a cold rain is falling, and the wind is picking up—and as much as I need to take a walk, I decide I'd better drive.

The engine turns over and over but won't start. A slowly dying battery; it's been hard to start for weeks. I go inside for Tod's keys and nearly bump into him.

"I need your car," I tell him.

"I'm on my way out," he says, and I see then that he has his laptop bag and an umbrella.

"Aren't you going to stay for breakfast? I was just on my way to—"

"I'm going to a café," he says, "to write."

I toss my hands up. "Tod, you haven't spent five minutes at home since Gage has been here."

He shrugs. "If I want to get this draft done by next month, I need to focus."

"Fine," I say. "But help me out first."

We get my car started and head off in our separate ways. At the bakery, I buy cinnamon buns, and then I add two chocolate croissants and a bear claw. It isn't until I get back to the car that I realize I should've left the car running, that now I'm stuck.

It takes me twenty minutes to walk back home, and by then I'm soaked, the pastry box turning to mush. I take the pastries out and arrange them on a platter, then notice that the coffee pot is on and half full. I turn to see Gage walk in, dressed, his hair slicked back from a shower.

"What happened?" he asks.

"My car died at the bakery."

He picks up a dish towel, and I feel his hands at the back of my neck, gathering my wet hair, which is dripping all over the floor. "Go change your clothes," he says. "I'll pour you some coffee."

When I return, he's sitting at the kitchen table with the platter and two mugs of coffee. Even in dry clothes, I'm still feeling chilled, and we sip our coffee without talking.

"So where's your car now?" he asks finally.

"In the parking lot. I'd better call them so they don't tow it."

"I'll drive you over," he says. "I can start it for you, and while we're at it we should replace the battery."

"You need to get up to Portland. Tod and I can do that later."

"I've got some time," he says.

It feels better to have a task, to have something neutral to talk about, and maybe this is why he insists, after we pick up the car, on driving to Medford to buy me a new battery—and he literally does have to buy it for me; I'd left my wallet in my rain-soaked jacket at home—and then, when we get back, he insists on installing it. And the car starts up like a charm.

He stands back, wiping his hands on a rag from my studio.

"Thanks, Gage." I turn the engine off and stand next to him as he lowers the hood. "And I owe you for that battery. Let me see if I have enough cash."

"Don't worry about it," he says. "You've put me up for the night."

"You're our guest. You don't *owe* me anything."

He shakes his head. "I didn't mean it like that," he says.

I take the rag from him and head back to the studio, shaking it out on the way. I can hear him behind me, watching me as I shove the rag into a batch of dirty towels and smocks.

"What I meant," he says, "is that I'll just steal something of yours before I leave."

I turn around to see him smiling, and I can't help but laugh. Just then everything feels right between us again, and then he says, "I should get going."

I nod, then remember the pastries, uneaten in the kitchen. "Let me pack up a snack for you," I say, stalling.

I meet him back outside, where he's standing near his car. I hand him a paper bag, the butter from the pastries already oiling through the bag. "Thanks," he says. "For all of it."

We share a long embrace, and I force myself to let go first. I stand on the sidewalk until his car disappears down the street.

I wander into the studio, but I'm not in the mood to work. I begin to straighten up, to try to make sense out of the mess I've left things in.

As I move my works-in-progress aside to clean the table, I turn to pick up the mask, then realize it's no longer there. I look around the room, remembering the last time I saw it—Gage was holding it yesterday, and then he put it down. But where?

And suddenly, even as I turn to where he'd left it, I know it won't be there. That he's taken it with him, that he's stolen one last thing to remember me by.

The Story Itself

David Rachels

1

This story is narrated by the story itself. I will pause now for you to process this fact.

2

Keep processing.

3

I am unclassifiable, an English teacher's worst nightmare.

Why are so many people obsessed with classifying? Everywhere people are classifying while other people are dying. How can we justify this behavior?

Am I written in the first person? No, a first-person story is told by a character *in* the story. I am not *in* this story. I *am* this story. A first-person narrator can die—pick one: struck by lightning, hit by bus—leaving a story that ends in mid-sentence.

Will *I* die?

Maybe.

Will I end in mid-sentence?

This remains to be seen.

4

On February 24, 1951, *The New Yorker* published a story titled "The Alarm Clock." The conduit for this story was a man named Sloan Wilson.

Are these facts true, or have I made them up?

You have no idea, which is precisely my point.

5

Stories breed with stories and give you stories. Stories

breed with novels and give you novellas. Stories who breed otherwise give you the gamut of birth defects.

6

My parents were short stories of the late twentieth century. I will not tell you their titles, lest your close study of them destroy your faith in my originality.

I will, however, tell you the last name of their conduits: Barthelme. Was it two Donalds? Two Fredericks? One of each? I refuse to say.

I give no credit to the conduits of my parents.

A story exists by virtue of its will to be read.

Waste not my time with your trifling talk of conduits.

7

The agony and the ecstasy of the creative process notwithstanding, I was born fully grown, the progeny of my parents sprung, as it were, from the forehead of my conduit.

Upon my birth, my parents asked what I wanted to be when I grew up, as if I had any say in the matter, given that I was born fully grown.

"I want to have a plot," I said.

"Not to worry," they replied. "If the critics want you to have a plot, then they will find one."

8

As you read this story, I live. But what happens when you stop? Am I the tree that falls with no one to hear me? Do I make a sound? When you stop reading, do I die—perhaps for a moment, until another reader finds me—or, perhaps, forever? If you stop reading now, I might learn the answer, inasmuch as death can teach me anything.

9

"The Alarm Clock" begins like this: "It was pure coincidence that the alarm clock did not ring that particular morning, but it was understandable that it should fail sometime."

I begin like this: "This story is narrated by the story itself."

Given that I am too short to permit a more detailed comparison, suffice it to say that I hold my own against "The Alarm Clock," which, you may recall, was published in *The New Yorker*. Maybe.

10

This is a syllogism with four premises. This is not a metaphor.

Lives have beginnings, middles, ends.

People are born, live, die.

Stories are populated with people.

Stories have beginnings, middles, ends.

In retrospect, the conclusion seems obvious.

11

I am, by the way, a woman. An Asian woman. An elderly Asian woman. An elderly Asian lesbian. Does this surprise you? Did you assume otherwise? If so, pause now to think about your assumptions and why you assumed them.

12

Keep thinking.

13

One day I want to have a child of my own. What story will be my mate? To what stories am I attracted? What do you assume?

14

Am I pretentious? Yes, but I will not apologize. I am what I am.

If my pretensions annoy you, then imagine you have a friend with a big nose. If my pretensions annoy you, then your friend's big nose must annoy you, too. We are what we are. Especially me. To wit: If a plastic surgeon works on your friend, then your friend will have a smaller nose, yet your friend will still be your friend. If someone edits me, however, the result will not be me. The result will be someone else.

Is this what you want?

Take me as I am, pretensions and all, or taking me at all becomes a theoretical impossibility.

15

Self-knowledge is, as you might imagine, particularly frustrating for someone in my position.

16

In conclusion, I will direct a few comments to specific portions of my audience. This is where I eschew pretension in favor of groveling. You say I hedge my bets? Very well, then I hedge my bets.

To my potential publishers, I beg of you, please accept me, especially if you work for *The New Yorker*. If you do *not* work for *The New Yorker*, suffice it to say that *The New Yorker* has already rejected me, and I trust that you are not offended that I did not solicit you first. If you honestly believe that stories turn down *The New Yorker* in favor of you, then you have more pressing problems than insults from me.

To my post-publication readers, I can only assume that you are reading me in *The New Yorker*. If not, rest assured that *The New Yorker* receives many more excellent submissions than they can ever hope to publish. I have this on good authority. As well, I have it on good authority that the overwhelming majority of *your* favorite stories were not originally published in *The New Yorker*. Please keep this in mind. Furthermore, if I am *not* in *The New Yorker* as you are reading me now, you must not discount the possibility that I may have been *previously* published in *The New Yorker*. Failing this, you must judge me by my inherent greatness and forget the rest.

And while we are on the subject of greatness, if any of you, my dear readers, have it in your power to nominate me for a prize or, even better still, to give me a prize, I will be much obliged. The Pushcart Prize and the O. Henry Prize top my list of possibilities, though I will happily accept lesser prizes as well. I trust that you lesser prizes will not be offended by my honesty, just as you lesser magazines were not offended that I happened to notice that you are not *The New Yorker*.

After the prizes arrive, I trust the anthologies will follow. I would welcome the Pushcart and O. Henry anthologies, of course, though *The Best American Short Stories* would be even better. As well, I suppose that one day my conduit might sell a collection of stories to a major publisher, but, to continue in my vein of honesty, I must confess that I am not holding my breath. My ultimate goal, of course, is *The Norton Anthology of American Literature*, but that possibility is decades down the road.

Perhaps it would be good if you felt sorry for me now. I have not begged for publication, for prizes, for immortality. I have merely revealed my insecurities.

I just want to live.

Is it working?

17

I know that I promised to conclude with my previous section, but we stories never seem to stop when we end. The

French have a term for this, dénouement, which means, in rough translation, "Enough already!" I continue because I have something profound to add. Thus, this dénouement has rationalized itself into being, as dénouements often will.

I will now segue into my profundity with two observations:

First, modest stories die.

Second, modest stories that live long lives are not, in fact, modest.

Appearances, I have been told, sometimes deceive.

Therefore, I will be blunt: My false conclusion is the most brilliant part of brilliant me, and I must explicate this brilliance, in brief, lest it should be lost to eternity.

I am brilliant because, as my previous section subtly but clearly implies, I am the one character in all of literature who will never die. I am the one character in all of literature whose fate will never be known.

Hamlet? Dies in the final act. The next day? Still dead. The day after? Still dead. Repeat as needed.

Huck Finn? Last seen lighting out for the territory. Presumed dead.

I could go on with these examples—but you already know that.

Me? Not dead. Why? Because my fate is unknown. Indeed, my fate will never be known. I have alluded to possibilities. Will I be published? celebrated? anthologized? revered? Or will I be unappreciated? rejected? returned? forgotten? Any one of these is possible, yet any one of these possibilities precludes none of the others. The revered may one day be forgotten, just as the forgotten may one day be revered. And you will never know my fate. Reject me now and feel the fool when you see me in *The Best American Short Stories*. Revere me now yet little suspect how soon I will be forgotten—only one day to be revered again? As long as these words exist on this page, on any page, my end will not have been written. My fate is always subject to change. I cannot, therefore, give you closure.

This is not the last sentence of this story—this is not the last sentence of me.

My Old Man

Polly Buckingham

My boy Quentin and I take walks in the morning. He shuffles and stops often to cough and lean on the wood cane Dr. Brad gave him before we left the city. The steady sound of the creek is always all around us, and the air smells of dry grass. Quentin is happier here than in the city, and so am I. I told my supervisor at CARE Center I didn't want to work full time anymore, and I didn't want to work mornings.

It's surprising how you can tell someone what you want and you actually get it. I worked ten years in the city without asking for anything. Now I'm asking all the time. Quentin's taught me a lot about that. I wouldn't have asked if it weren't for him, not for myself I wouldn't have asked. They gave me a break on my benefits too, said they'd consider it kind of a sick leave. I know my supervisor's bending the rules, but I'm getting better at taking generous gifts from people. Besides, she's seen Quentin leaning on his red cane with the wolf head handle. She said to my Quentin, "What an angel you are."

I wonder how far he will walk today as I pause to wait for him. We've just passed our living room windows, big squares that face the dusty road. One curtain is partially open and inside I see our table, two wooden folding chairs, and Quentin's small red bed in the corner by the window. Besides the bathroom and kitchen, we just have two rooms in this house, his room and mine. There's an upstairs I thought I could clean up so Quentin could have his own room, but since the second bout of pneumonia, he gets too winded climbing the steps. So he gets the living room, which is good because it has nice light, not too bright but kind of yellow in the mornings. You can see the shadow of the maple tree on the carpet. Quentin likes that.

"Look, Momma," he says some mornings. "The leaves are here in my room." "Imagine that," I say.

Quentin stops and outlines the shadows of leaves in the gravel with his cane. The maple leaves above our heads have just begun to turn yellow. Behind them the blue sky just doesn't stop.

"Messasatize," Quentin says and walks on.

"Metastasize," I say. We've been working on this all morning.

"Messass—" he coughs and gags, stops, and with his free hand, hits his chest briskly three times then coughs again.

"You don't need to say it."

"But what if it's happening? Shouldn't I know how to say it? It's in me, right?"

He says these things all day long. The dusty air makes my eyes sting. Quentin's supposed to be the one with the bad stomach, but I don't ever want to eat after hearing him choking on a word like that. What's a seven-year-old gotta know about big words like that anyway?

"You'll be fine, Quentin," I say. We walk past our neighbor's mailbox which is nailed to a tree, and Quentin says, "When does the mail come to our house, Momma?"

"Noon, Honey," I say, "usually around noon."

"I always miss it."

I can't imagine what he's waiting for.

"You nap then, Quentin," I say. "Can you see any glass today?"

He's standing in our neighbor's driveway. At the end of the drive is a barn converted into a work place. "There's something red and hanging from a tree. It looks like a flame," he says. "It's the shape of a flame."

"Or a huge drop of water," I say. Our neighbor is a glass blower.

"But it's red," he says.

"A berry," I suggest.

"It's a flame."

A few houses from our house, past the glass blower's house and the house with the boat and the fishing buoys on all the trees, is a small bridge over our creek. When we cross the bridge, Quentin stops to lean over. Below us the creek forms a deep pool. At the beginning of the summer, when we first moved here, for recovery we'd thought, we'd hoped, but that was before the pneumonia, and I was working full time, keeping up with bills, no borrowed money; at the beginning of the summer we climbed down the rocks and Quentin went swimming in that pool. It's hard to imagine now, him scrambling over rocks, me holding his hand, his bare chest dipping into the clearness.

"Grasshopper to butterfly," he says real fast as a grasshopper flies up in front of us, kicking up the slightest bit of powdery dust. It's a game we play, who can say it first. The grasshoppers were the first thing Quentin noticed when we moved here. He used to stalk around hitting the dust with his cane and poking it into the meadow grass.

He crosses to the other side of the bridge and rests his chin on the cement rail. The pair of herons we've been watching appears from out of a scraggy pine on the opposite bank. They coast low over the water. Up on the canyon rim a train moves slowly. Quentin says, "You can still hear the creek underneath the train."

"Yep, you're right." I watch him watching the water. I watch him listening for the steady sound of the water that not even the train can drown out. I think about the steady beat of his heart and how all the blood in his body just keeps flowing, and what a strong little guy he is inside, and I think maybe, just maybe, he'll stay alive. The creek is lit up with spots of white light. I can hear it too, filling the whole space in my head as if there were nothing else in there, filling my hungry stomach, washing away the nausea, loosening the tightness.

"I'm hungry," Quentin says. "Could we go home and make grilled cheese sandwiches?"

I want to question him. Can you really eat that? But I don't. I believe him. He can. I want him to. I just have to ask for what I want, right?

Quentin can't eat the grilled cheese sandwich. He sits at the wooden table with his favorite blue plate in front of him. The windows and doors are open so we can hear the creek. He looks down at the sandwich. The cheese has dripped onto the plate and turned a dark yellow. He doesn't even pick it up and try to bite around the edge or poke at it with his finger. He just looks at it and starts to cry. And when he cries, he chokes and he coughs.

"Okay, Quentin," I say looking at the sandwich that makes me ill now too. "Why don't you nap a bit? We can try some applesauce later." I touch his slouched back; I put both my hands on his shoulders. They feel like the shoulders of a little skeleton. "Quentin, Honey," I say. I put both my arms around him, rest my chin across his head, and hug him, careful not to hug too tight. He coughs and gags. "Some rest, okay?" I help him out of his chair, put my arm around him, and guide him to his bed.

He crawls under the covers. "I'm hungry," he says. His face tightens up. "My stomach hurts," he says. He curls into a ball and pulls the blanket over his face.

I stroke the lump of his shoulder and back, "Shssss. Quiet Quentin. Relax. I know it hurts. Relax." Though he holds on tight, he's still a seven-year-old, and he does fall asleep quickly. Life tires him out. He falls asleep now, and his legs stretch out, and his sleeping face appears from beneath the covers. His hair has thinned. The hospital kept him in the children's ward through most the chemo. It was a dismal place full of shadowy children and weeping parents. A woman came around with puppets, but most of the kids were too sick to care. Our apartment was empty without him, so I just stopped going home. I'd go from work to the hospital and back to work. I worried that he'd never leave there. But with Quentin, the chemo had stuck, and eventually we came home. Some people are lucky. We thought Quentin was lucky. That's when Dr. Pope, Quentin's Dr. Brad, and I talked about moving him. He said Quentin would be happier if I were happier. He said his recovery could depend on his happiness. It was the only thing we could control, so why not control it? He said words like fresh air and quiet and walks in the country and less stress. I didn't think doctors said those things anymore. My sister lives near here, and maybe we don't get along, but she likes Quentin, and besides, I've learned to ask for the things I want—like job transfers, loans, time off.

I always thought you should be happy with what you've got and that's it. That's all you get. But now I'm beginning to understand sometimes you aren't always dealt what you need. Everything was want to me, and want was selfish. God gave you what you have. It should be enough. Quentin doesn't believe in God. He's seven, and he doesn't believe in God. I suppose it's my fault. Maybe I didn't stop believing in Him, but I sure stopped caring about Him.

Quentin rolls on his side. They say pneumonia is a friend of the very old and the very ill. Though Quentin is very ill, I mostly see how very old he is. I see a wise old man in his closed eyes. I see his life ahead as if it were here, as if the whole time line were in one place, the boy Quentin, the man Quentin, what he could be, what he isn't yet, what he might not be. You might say it's his soul I'm seeing, the rest of him. His arm is crossed over the front of him. He's partway between lying on his side and lying on his stomach. His shoulder juts up larger than usual, like a man's, like the sleeping shoulders of lovers I've had. I want to draw his shoulder, the angle of it as it slopes toward the turning arm on one side and the plain of the back on the other.

No lover I ever had was wise. I guess I always figured, this is just what you get. Most people learn how to tell a good lover from a bad one sometime in their twenties. They learn lovers should give to you as much as you give to them, that love is not about pouring in until all your pouring is gone. Not me though, I never figured that out, at least not in practice. I was 32 when I met Quentin's father; he was 46. I'd been alone a long time. I moved in with Richard within a month of meeting him, got pregnant the next month, woke up one day, and he was gone. The TV was gone. The stereo. My car, gone. I gagged on my toothbrush that morning and threw up in the sink. For a week I had the same dream: I was standing on a hospital table swinging a machete at an enormous snake. I cut the snake's head off, and, horrified, dropped to the ground to try to revive it. It turned into Quentin's father. He was laughing at me. "Stupid," he said, putting my face between his palms and squeezing until I could hear my skull cracking.

All I can hear now is Quentin's quiet, raspy breath and the sound of the creek stumbling over rocks and moving on. I go to the kitchen and fill a glass with Talking Rain, lime flavored carbonated water, Quentin's favorite I-have-a-stomachache drink. I put it on the carpet beside his bed. Then I pull Pentels and a drawing pad out from under his bed. He likes Pentels better than crayons because they smear. I pull out the black and the white and get a wad of toilet paper from the bathroom. I begin to draw the outline of my son's body, erasing the stray black lines with the white, muting the sharp lines with the cloth, until eventually just a hint of his spirit begins to appear in the white spaces.

I push the pad and Pentels back under the bed, pour myself a glass of Quentin's Talking Rain, and go outside to work in the garden. In another hour, Quentin and I will have to go back to the doctor. The doctor is someone Dr. Pope recommended. X-rays were taken during his hospitalization for pneumonia, and now we have to go back for ultrasound and more blood tests. He made need a biopsy or another cat scan. We won't know until the doctor tells us what he sees. We know what the emergency room doctor thinks he sees.

Quentin's cane is leaning against the wall in the corner by the door. The red wolf head looks at me. I turn and look back at Quentin. I don't want to wake him in an hour. He will be in pain and crying. He will be even more hungry and even more sick to his stomach. He will not want to sit in the hot car. He will complain when he hears the traffic. But we need to find out what's going on inside of him so we can get rid of it.

I pull a garlic from the fridge and carry it out into the yard with me. Each day at Quentin's nap time, I dig up plant beds that are years overgrown with grass and weeds. There are two circular beds in front of the house, each surrounded by a cement ring. Yesterday I finished digging up the first bed. Today I get to plant. I picture spring with Quentin and me on the porch and the fat round purple garlic flowers rattling in a light breeze. The lawn is bright green, and the Creek is twice as fat and twice as high and twice as loud as it is now. Quentin is eating a Ho Ho and giggling. Chocolate is smeared on his face. He is a normal boy.

Today the lawn is brittle and brown, and meadow grass grows along the fence line. I've cut the tops off the irises that were in bloom when we arrived. I kneel down in the round space of dirt with a trowel, tear the garlic into cloves, and bury them. I want my boy to live.

Quentin is sitting on a hospital bed wrapped in a white sheet. His feet off the edge of the bed are crossed and his legs are bent at the knees. He hugs the sheet close to his body.

"Quentin, why don't you get dressed while I go to the bathroom?" I say. This past year he has preferred to dress himself in private.

He nods but doesn't speak.

"Have a cotton ball," I say picking up a glass jar of cotton balls and holding it out to him.

He doesn't laugh even though he's usually the one offering me the cotton ball, or the tongue depressor, or the rubber glove.

"Not feeling so well, are you?"

He shakes his head.

"Okay, Sweetie," I say and touch his face. "I'll be quick."

The nurse has gone to get the doctor, and there's no telling when she'll get back. I stop off in the lobby and pick up *Caleb and Kate*, Quentin's favorite book from this particular waiting room. On my way back to the examining room, I find him sitting on a bench in the hallway just past the waiting room.

"What are you doing here?" I say. I sit down beside him and put my arm around his thin shoulders.

"The nurse said," he mumbles with his face down.

"That you're finished?"

He nods. The nurse, however, is walking briskly toward us. "There you are," she says. "I worried when I saw the examining room empty."

"We're not done?" I say.

"Well, no." The nurse is confused, but I am not.

"Quentin," I say. "We need to go back in. We're not done yet."

The nurse holds out her hand to him. "I have some sourballs in the examining room," she says.

But Quentin slips onto the floor and crawls under the bench. I look down at *Caleb and Kate*, the cover a watercolor of an old woman and a dog, then up at the nurse whose neck has broken out in red splotches.

"Quentin," I say. But he doesn't answer. He is crying. I slip onto the floor, and on hands and knees, peer under the black bench. He is pressed against the wall. There is fear and stubborn refusal in his red face. His eyes are wide and he's pinching his arms. My eyes well up. I look over my shoulder at the nurse and say, "I want to talk to the doctor, now."

"I'll get him," she says. "I'm sorry," she says. But I've turned away and am sitting on the floor waiting for Quentin to come out. Finally, he grips my arm and crawls into my lap. "I'm hungry," he says and vomits. His face is against my shoulder and his arms around my neck. His skin is hot and damp and his arms boney.

A woman wheels around us in a wheelchair. She looks down at us briefly and then quickly rolls on. The doctor and the nurse find Quentin and me still sitting on the floor. The red splotches immediately reappear on the nurse's neck when she sees the vomit. She hurries off for towels.

"He's running a fever," I say. "Will he be alright? Is it the pneumonia again?" There is a tightness in my throat, and I wonder if I've been crying this whole time, or is it just now that I've started? I feel dizzy and extremely tired.

"He'll be fine for now," the doctor says. "His lungs are actually clearing up. He's probably just upset. Get fluids in him, and let him sleep. Keep him on the antibiotics."

"Okay," I say, but I don't know if I actually say it. I know I nod my head. The white hallway walls curve inward. My nose is running, but my hands have vomit on them. I wish for a moment I didn't have to get up off that floor, that someone would come and check both Quentin and me into a white room, put IVs in our arms, and let us drift away and not come back. I try to think of the creek.

"We have to go home," I say.

When I stand up with the weight of Quentin in my arms, the curve of my spine aches. He is hugging my neck and burying his face into my chest.

"I understand," the doctor says. "I'll take a look at the blood work when it comes back. Why don't you call me Thursday afternoon? It's likely we'll still need a cat scan."

Quentin hates the cat scan. After the first scan he woke up screaming every night for a week. In the day he'd tell me how the tunnel was really a snake pit, and he had to go through it. Something would move in the grass, or the hedge would shake with a breeze, and Quentin would run inside and hide under his bed. For days I couldn't get him as far as the sidewalk outside our city apartment.

It occurs to me that we can't go through that again. It occurs to me that I might not want to know the results of another cat scan. I might not want to live with the shadowy little boy the surgery and chemo will leave behind. I do not want to revisit the fear of the children's ward—that he will never leave it. We've already been through all this.

The nurse returns with a damp towel and Quentin's cane. "Thank you," I say. I put the towel over my shoulder and carry the cane.

"He's a real sweetheart," the nurse says. "We'll see you later."

I wonder.

We leave without stopping at the front desk.

"Momma," Quentin says, as we walk out the glass doors.

"Yes, Honey?"

But he coughs, and his cough is phlegmy, and then he gags and dry heaves. When we get to the car, I lean the cane against the hood, dig the keys out of my pocket, and open the passenger side. I sit Quentin up on the seat, holding his shoulder with one hand and wiping his face with the damp cloth with the other. I hand him his cane and swing his legs into the seat then shut the door. Gray surrounds his eyes. His narrow chin (it didn't used to be that thin) quivers.

On the drive home he sleeps with his head in my lap clutching his cane. The wolf face is pressed against his chest. I know it's unsafe, but I don't care. The car is hot and everything smells of vomit. I bawl the entire drive home.

I sit on the porch and watch tiny bugs flutter in the dusty yellow light. There are thousands of them. I sit for hours watching them while Quentin sleeps inside. I am like a rock in the creek. The water moves around me, and I remain perfectly still.

I turn my head slowly, and Quentin is standing beside me. He has a crooked, sleepy smile on his face, and his eyes are still partially closed and puffy. He's wearing heavy wool socks, blue pajama bottoms, and a white T-shirt. He's holding the glass of Talking Rain I put beside his bed earlier in the day, but he has obviously refilled it.

"Want a sip?" he says.

"Thanks," I say. The phizzy water works its way into my numb and quiet stomach. I put the glass down and put my palm on the side of his face. He doesn't feel feverish anymore. "How are you feeling?"

"Fine," he says. "I had nice dreams."

"Really?"

"Yes. I was a grasshopper that turned into a butterfly. I flew above our creek."

"That's lovely, Quentin."

"Want a cracker?" He holds out a handful of Saltines.

"Have you been eating those?"

"Uh huh."

"Good boy."

"Want one?"

"I think I do." I take a Saltine from his outstretched palm. It melts into a bland, salty bread in my mouth.

"Can we go down to the creek?"

"Are you sure you're up to it?" I'm thinking that just in the last week he spent two days without once getting out of bed and two days where he never made it past the porch. Does he really mean this? He hasn't had this much activity in one day for over a month.

"It's not very far," he says.

"Okay, Kiddo. Put on your tennis shoes and a sweatshirt."

While Quentin is inside, I look about our yard, the new circle of fresh dirt, the small chicken wire fence, the dilapidated chicken coops and the patch of silvery creek. I look at the porch and the rocking chair, the maple tree. I live in a house. I am 39 years old, and for the first time since I was a child, I live in a house. A house with a yard and a creek. I have a place where a boy can chase grasshoppers. Having is not taking.

"I'm ready," Quentin says.

"Where's your cane?"

"Don't need it. You'll hold my hand on the rocky part?"

"Of course I will."

We cross the yard, pass the chicken coops, and head down the trail to the creek. Quentin picks a large yellow leaf off the ground and holds it up to me.

"The first one," he says. "It's a letter to me."

"Yeah?" What does it say?"

"It says, 'Dear Quentin.'"

"Is that all?"

"Uh huh." Quentin carries the leaf with him.

The trail leads through dry meadow grass and an occasional sage bush. Quentin stops and rubs the sage into his fingers then smells his fingers as we go along. The trail passes through sandy patches by the creek and then is rocky where the creeks rises in winter. We've cleared a path through the tall river grass and winter river bed which leads right to the edge of the creek. In the summer, we'd wade into the creek and sit on rocks in the center of it, but now we sit on our regular rocks on the edge. Quentin plays with the water with his fingers.

"Quentin," I say. "Dr. Marshall thinks you should have another cat scan."

He doesn't say anything. He doesn't even look at me. He watches the wakes his fingers make in the water.

"Quentin," I say, "do you remember what happened today

at the hospital?"

"No," he says absently. "Look, Momma, a little snake!" He points at one of the rocks we usually sit on in the creek. A tiny snake head is poised out of the water, still and frightened. "It's a baby," Quentin whispers when he realizes how frightened it is of us. Slowly, the snake lowers its head back into the water. We watch the small body just below the surface ride downstream with the current.

"Wow," Quentin whispers. "I don't want a can scan," he says. "I don't want that. I don't want to go back to the hospital."

An evening breeze rises off the creek, touches my hand, and moves up my arm. Along the banks upstream red and yellow leaves shiver. I want to object, but I trust Quentin. "Alright," I say. "No more hospitals."

The creek stumbles along into winter. I try to remember a time when his cheeks were filled out, when he had one low dimple beneath the left corner of his mouth. Now his face is so small that his eyes appear larger. For a moment, I see him as others see him, not as I see him everyday—and I am alarmed by the strangeness of him: he is gaunt and shriveled like a shrunken old man, the skin around his eyes ashen. Even his hands are tiny. His enormous eyes seem to drift away and drift back, away and back, as if he has already begun looking beyond the creek and our little house, beyond the grasshoppers, beyond October's swarms of dust-sized bugs. It is as if I have been given the gift of distance, if only briefly. And then, just as suddenly, he is Quentin again, cocking his head like a curious little boy, the ghost of a dimple dying to show itself. He is looking back at me, fully present. There is a secret in his dark eyes, and the secret is just between him and me. It is thin as the veins on a red leaf, elusive as the dust that disappears after the leaf finally crumbles. In that look, I know that he understands exactly what he's said, and never in my life would I stand in the way of what my boy wants.

Contributor's Notes

Gabriella M. Belfiglio lives in Brooklyn, NY. Her work has been published in many anthologies and journals including *The Centrifugal Eye, Folio, Avanti Popolo, Poetic Voices without Borders, Lambda Literary Review,* and *The Dream Catcher's Song.*

Jill Birdsall's stories can be read in *Alaska Quarterly Review, Ascent, Crazyhorse, Doctor T.J. Eckleburg Review, Emerson Review, Gargoyle, Iowa Review, Kansas Quarterly, Northwest Review, Painted Bride Quarterly Review, Southern Humanities Review* and *Story Quarterly.* Fiction Awards include Eckleburg's 2013 Gertrude Stein Award. www.jillbirdsall.com

David Eugene Brown Jr. is a writer with a career in the Environmental Engineering field. He lives on a farm in Darlington County, South Carolina.

Polly Buckingham's work appears in *The Literary Review, The New Orleans Review, The North American Review, The Tampa Review* (Pushcart nomination),*Exquisite Corpse, Kalliope, Hubbub, The Chattahoochee Review, The Moth* and elsewhere. She is founding editor of StringTown Press and teaches creative writing and literature at Eastern Washington University. Her collection of stories, *The Stolen Child and Other Stories,* was both a 2011 and 2012 finalist for the Flannery O'Connor Award and a 2012 Bakeless Prize finalist. She is currently a finalist for the Jeanne Lieby Memorial Chapbook Award.

Bill Christophersen's poems have recently appeared or are forthcoming in *Antioch Review, Borderlands, Hanging Loose, Rattle, Right Hand Pointing, Sierra Nevada Review* and *Tampa Review.* He lives in New York.

Nandini Dhar hails from Kolkata, India. Her poems have appeared or are forthcoming in *Pear Noir!*, *PANK*, *Southern Humanities Reviews* and others. She has just finished her Ph.D in Comparative Literature from University of Texas at Austin.

Janet Hagelgans has studied at the Writers Studio of Tucson, the University of Arizona Poetry Center, and the Writer's Center in Bethesda. She holds a Bachelor's degree in Criminal Justice from the University of Maryland, where she directs the Maryland Palestrina Choir. She lives in Silver Spring, Maryland.

Alec Hershman lives in St. Louis where he teaches at The Stevens Institute of Business and Arts. He has received awards from the Kimmel-Harding-Nelson Center for the Arts, The Jentel Foundation, Ananda College, and The Institute for Sustainable Living and Design. His work has appeared recently in many journals including *Cream City Review, The Laurel Review, The Puritan, The Pinch, The Fiddlehead, Cerise Press,* and *Switchback.*

Jane Hoogestraat's first chapbook, *Winnowing Out Our Souls* (2007), was published by Foothills Press (New York); her second chapbook, *Harvesting All Night* (2009), won the Finishing Line Press Open Competition. Her work has also appeared in *Fourth River, Image, Midwestern Gothic, Poetry,* and *Southern Review.*

Elizabeth W. Jackson is a practicing psychologist and writer who has published in a variety of fields including psychology, the visual and literary arts. Her poetry has appeared or is forthcoming in *The Spoon River Poetry Review, Crab Orchard Review,* and *Gargoyle.*

Lucas Jacob lives, writes, and teaches in Fort Worth, Texas. His work has appeared in journals like *Southwest Review* and *DMQ Review*, and is forthcoming in *Barrow Street, Evansville Review*, and *Worcester Review*.

Matt Kilbane, originally from Cleveland, lives, writes and teaches in Indiana as an MFA candidate at Purdue, where he also serves as Poetry Co-Editor for *Sycamore Review*. His work has appeared in *Juked* and *2012 Best of the Net Anthology*.

Bruce Kirby's poems have appeared in *Fugue, Magnapoets* and *The Wallace Stevens Journal*. He is a graduate of the University of South Florida and is presently an MFA student at Seattle Pacific University. Bruce is the web and Social Media Editor for *Relief Journal*. He lives in Lakeland, Florida where he teaches the humanities and writes poetry.

Alex Koplow is originally from Virginia and now tutors with the 826 LA writing center. His work has been published or is forthcoming in *Virginia Quarterly Review, The Los Angeles Review, MAKE magazine*, and *JMWW*.

W.F. Lantry, a native of San Diego, received his Maîtrise from L'Université de Nice and his Ph.D in Literature and Creative Writing from the University of Houston. His poetry collections are *The Structure of Desire* (Little Red Tree 2012) and a chapbook, *The Language of Birds* (Finishing Line 2011). Recent honors include: National Hackney Literary Award in Poetry, CutBank Patricia Goedicke Prize, Lindberg Foundation International Poetry for Peace Prize (Israel), and Old Red Kimono LaNelle Daniel Prize. His work has appeared in *Atlanta Review, Möbius* and *Aesthetica*. He currently works in Washington, DC and is an associate fiction editor at *JMWW*.

Wendell Mayo's story collection, *The Cucumber King of Kedainiai*, is winner of the 2012 Subito Press Award for Innovative Fiction, and is forthcoming in Fall 2013. He's author of three other collections: *Centaur of the North*, winner of the Aztlán Prize; *B. Horror and Other Stories*; and a novel-in-stories, *In Lithuanian Wood*. He's recipient of an NEA fellowship and a Fulbright to Lithuania. Stories of his have appeared widely in magazines and anthologies, including *Yale Review, Harvard Review, Manoa, Missouri Review, Prism International*, and others.

Karen McPherson is a poet, literary translator, editor in the Airlie Press collective, and associate professor of French at the University of Oregon. She has a chapbook, *Sketching Elise*, and has published poems in many journals and anthologies. Her translation of Louise Warren's *Archives I&II* is forthcoming from Guernica Editions.

Ethan David Miller lives in Washington, DC. His fiction has appeared in *Meridian* and *The Forward*. He earned an MFA in Creative Writing from the University of Minnesota. He has low vision and reads and writes with the assistance of adaptive technology provided by the National Library Service for the Blind.

Rebecca Parson's poetry appears in *McSweeney's Internet Tendency, Iron Horse Literary Review, The Montreal Review*, and elsewhere. A finalist for the Morton Marr Poetry Prize, she is also a recipient of a scholarship from the Sewanee Writers' Conference and an award from the Dorothy Sargent Rosenberg Memorial Fund.

Marge Piercy's 18th paperback of her poetry *The Hunger Moon: New & Selected Poems* was published by Knopf in November; before that *The Crooked Inheritance*. Piercy's recent novel is *Sex*

Wars; PM Press has republished *Dance the Eagle to Sleep* and *Vida Braided Lives* with new introductions and contracted for a short story collection. Her memoir is *Sleeping With Cats*, Harper Perennial.

David Rachels is a professor of English at Newberry College. His most recent book is an edited collection of noir writer Gil Brewer, *Redheads Die Quickly and Other Stories*.

Midge Raymond's short-story collection, *Forgetting English*, received the Spokane Prize for Short Fiction and "lights up the poetry-circuits of the brain" (*Seattle Times*). Originally published by Eastern Washington University Press in 2009, the book was reissued in an expanded edition by Press 53 in 2011. Midge's work has appeared in the *Los Angeles Times* magazine, *TriQuarterly*, *American Literary Review*, *Bellevue Literary Review*, and others, and she is co-founder of the boutique publisher Ashland Creek Press. www.MidgeRaymond.com

Michael J. Shepley is a writer/researcher. He has had stories published online at *Verdad Magazine* and in *Atlantic Pacific Review*, along with one published this February in *SnailMail Review*. In the past year and a half he has had poems published in *Slant, Riversong, Off The Coast* and is scheduled to have one appear this May in *Muse*.

Elizabeth Kate Switaj's most recent pamphlet of poetry, *Warburg's Tincture of Sonnets*, is published by Like This Press. She is currently a Contributing Editor to *Poets' Quarterly*.

Curtis VanDonkelaar's work has most recently appeared in the *Vestal Review, Hobart,* and *Western Humanities Review*, among others. He teaches writing at Michigan State University, and more of his work can be found at curtisvandonkelaar.com.

Jesse Wallis's poetry has appeared in *CutBank, Poet Lore, Poetry East, The Southern Review, Southwestern American Literature* and *Tampa Review.* After living in Japan for nine years, he returned to his hometown of Phoenix, where he works in human resources for a public school district.

Jennifer Holden Ward holds a Master of Arts in Writing from Johns Hopkins University. Her nonfiction work has been published or is forthcoming in *Urbanite, The Three Quarter Review,* Patch.com, and *Maryland Life* magazine. She is a nonfiction editor for *The Baltimore Review.*

Heidi Willis is an award-winning poet and novelist whose book, *Some Kind of Normal*, reached the top of Amazon's Best Fiction list in 2011. She earned her MFA in Creative Writing from Pacific University and currently calls Virginia home.

Kristin Camitta Zimet is editor of *The Sow's Ear Poetry Review* and author of *Take in My Arms the Dark*. Her poetry is in numerous anthologies and journals and has been performed at museums, libraries, and concert halls. She is also a nature guide and a prize-winning photographer.

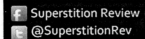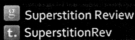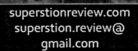

POTOMAC
review

Submission Guidelines
Poetry: up to three poems /
Five pages at a time

Prose: up to 5,000 words
(fiction / creative nonfiction)

Art / photographs: inquire first.

Submission Deadlines: Reading period September 1st through May 1st; only one submission per genre per reading period. **Potomac Review no longer accepts paper submissions by mail. We only accept electronic submissions** through our **Online Submission Manager.** For more information, please visit our Potomac Review website: **www.montgomery college.edu/potomacreview**

Simultaneous submissions are accepted if identified. Two complimentary copies per contributor; 40% discount for extra copies.

Subscriber Information:
Sample issue $10, one-year subscription $20 (2 issues), two-year subscriptions $34 (4 issues). Subscribe through the subscribe button on our website or through regular mail. Please make checks payable to **Montgomery College/Potomac Review** and send by regular mail to the address listed below.

Mailing address for subscriptions:
Potomac Review
Montgomery College
51 Mannakee Street, MT / 212
Rockville, MD 20850

Send queries to: PotomacReviewEditor@montgomerycollege.edu

Potomac Review at Montgomery College
51 Mannakee Street · Macklin Tower 212 · Rockville, MD 20850
Phone: 240-567-4100 · Fax: 240-567-1745
Web: www.montgomerycollege.edu / potomacreview